That night Leah lay on top of her bed with the light on, unable to sleep. To think that just this morning she had actually believed, no matter what had gone wrong with Chrissy, no matter how guilty she felt about leaving her mom, she was going to get into SFBA and that all the tears and fears would be worth it. Now she wondered how anyone actually got into the school. What did the judges look for in a fifteen-year-old girl? Good training? A strong, slim body? Charisma? Presence? Quality? Line? All the things that added up to talent? Leah didn't know. Pam said talent didn't count—not that much. But if talent didn't count, what did?

Leah rolled over onto her stomach and flicked out the light at last. She slipped between the crisp, clean sheets, hugged her knees to her chest, and asked herself one more time. Was there anything about her that would make her one of Madame Preston's chosen few?

TO BE
A DANCER
Satin Slippers #1

Elizabeth Bernard

FAWCETT GIRLS ONLY • NEW YORK

VL: Grades 7 + up
RLI:——————————
IL: Grades 8 + up

A Fawcett Girls Only Book
Published by Ballantine Books
Copyright © 1987 by Cloverdale Press, Inc.

Library of Congress Catalog Card Number: 87-90860

ISBN 0-449-13299-4

Manufactured in the United States of America

First Edition: October 1987

With special thanks to Capezio by Balletmakers and Gilda Mark for Flexitard.

To Dorothy Hill, my teacher,
and
Antoinette Sibley and Anthony Dowell,
whose partnership continues to inspire my own art

    Leah Stephenson glided across the floor of the Hannah Greene School of Dance and Theater Arts, trying not to cry. Leah had been one of Hannah Greene's star ballet students for nearly eight years now, and she hadn't ever cried in class: Not when she broke a bone in her foot the first time she wore pointe shoes; not when Annie MacPhearson got the part of the Sugar Plum Fairy in the school recital three years ago and Leah had to dance a dumb variation dressed up like a cello; not even when she was nine years old and her father died and she had come to her ballet lesson the day after his funeral and the other little girls were afraid to look her in the eye.

    No, she hadn't cried in front of Miss Greene. Not yet. Annie MacPhearson had cried plenty though. Every time the teacher yelled at her, she had squeezed out crocodile tears to get sympathy. And she had cried real tears of joy two years ago when she found out she had been accepted at New York City's School of American Ballet. She was just fourteen then, a year younger than Leah was now.

At the front of the room Leah came off pointe and scurried out of the way of the line of girls crossing the studio in one of the last pointe exercises of the day. Next to the old upright piano, Miss Greene sat straight and tall on a high wooden stool and shouted over the roar of a truck downshifting outside on Main Street.

"Pavlova's bourrées were no louder than a whisper. *Did you hear me? A whisper!*" Leah hurried past the dark-haired teacher, but Miss Greene seemed to look right through her. Today she had barely said a word to Leah. She hadn't even bothered to correct her once. Leah headed for the rosin box in the back of the room, her dark blue eyes bright with tears.

She dipped first the right toe of her worn pink satin shoes in the shallow wooden packing crate filled with chunks of sticky resin, then the left. *My whole life's about to fall apart and there's nothing I can do to stop it,* she thought. She leaned against the barre and stared out the curtained storefront window onto San Lorenzo's sleepy Main Street.

Today was the end of what Leah felt was the worst summer of her life. Six days a week for nearly two months the fifteen-year-old had danced her heart out in the sweltering studio. And six days a week, without fail, Miss Greene had singled her out for correction after correction, as if she were the only girl in the crowded room; as if, Leah recollected now, she were the worst dancer there.

At first Leah had appreciated the attention. After all, to be a dancer, a *great* dancer, was her most cherished dream. It had been her dream since the moment she put on her first pair of pink leather ballet slippers and walked into Hannah Greene's San Lorenzo dance studio when she was seven years old.

Leah was old enough now to realize her ambitions meant more than being singled out to give demonstrations and show the other girls how the more difficult combinations were supposed to look. Becoming a ballerina meant working very hard, harder than any of the other students currently in the advanced summer workshop. But Leah hadn't minded working hard as long as she knew someday her dream of dancing professionally would come true.

Lately that dream had seemed more like a nightmare. Miss Greene hadn't said one positive thing to her all summer. Nothing Leah did lately seemed to be right, or good enough, and she had begun to wonder if she should just give up. Perhaps it was her teacher's subtle way of telling her her days as a dancer were over.

Leah found Miss Greene's silence far worse than her shouted corrections. Today before class had started the teacher had approached Leah at the barre and said simply, "I want to see you in my office after class." Leah thought she knew what was coming. *She's going to tell me to stop dancing.* The thought had tumbled around in Leah's head all morning, blotting out everything else: the heat, the music, the steps, the other girls.

Now class was nearly over and Leah mentally prepared herself for the inevitable—the shattering of her dream. She bent over and rested her hot forehead against the worn wooden barre. "She's really going to tell me to stop dancing," Leah murmured in a soft, shocked voice.

"What do you mean, stop dancing?" Her best friend, Chrissy Morely, was standing beside her in the back of the room, wiping the sweat off her freckled face with a shocking-pink towel. The beginning pointe students were still doing steps in groups of two or three across the floor.

Leah straightened up and blinked. Chrissy's puzzled expression came into focus. Leah hadn't meant to speak her thoughts out loud. She looked down at the floor, rubbed the toe of one frayed shoe against the top of the other, and gave an embarrassed shrug. "Oh, I don't know exactly." Leah's shaky voice betrayed her. To steady herself, she clutched the barre that ran the length of the mirrored room. She worked one ankle round and round in a circle and studied her well-pointed foot closely. Without glancing up, she finally added under her breath, "You know how Greene's been treating me. Well, she wants to see me after class. In her office."

Chrissy had been studying with Hannah Greene almost as long as Leah had, but she had no intention of becoming a dancer. She wanted to be a veterinarian, but her mother kept insisting she take all these lessons: ballet, violin, pottery. Chrissy hated them. At the moment Leah envied her. If only there were something else she wanted to do with her life besides dance, she wouldn't feel so terrible now. She squeezed her eyes shut to hold back the tears. When she opened them again, she looked directly at her friend.

"She wants to see you in her office?" Chrissy's brown eyes widened as Leah's news registered. "Whew!" She gave a low, sympathetic whistle and pushed her red bangs out of her eyes. It was rare for one of the students to get called into Miss Greene's office. It usually happened only when they had a serious problem or were hurt. Chrissy patted Leah's arm. "Maybe it's not *bad* news," she said without much conviction.

On and off all summer Chrissy and Leah had hashed out Miss Greene's attitude toward Leah. At first they believed the stern, dark-haired teacher was trying to push Leah harder. After all, at fifteen a girl with her sights set on a professional dance career was ready for some kind of big move, and in Leah's case that meant a move out of the small-town world of San Lorenzo into one of the major big-city ballet schools—a move like the one Annie had made. First Annie had gone to New York to study. Now there was a letter from her posted on the dressing room bulletin board: she had been signed on as an apprentice at the New York City Ballet. She was almost two years older than Leah and Leah was beginning to wonder if she had been passed over. Lately Leah had begun to share her doubts with Chrissy. Maybe Miss Greene was trying to tell her something. Maybe she was built all wrong for dancing. Maybe she just wasn't good enough. Maybe that's why she was still here and Annie wasn't.

Leah's lip began to tremble and she didn't trust her voice. If she said one more word, she'd burst into tears.

"I'll wait for you after class," Chrissy whispered.

Leah nodded and turned her back on her friend. She made a big business of looking in the mirror and tucking a strand of thick blond hair back into her bun. For a moment she froze, with one hand on her head, and stared at her reflection as if she were looking at a perfect stranger. As she had a hundred times that summer, she took a hard critical look at her body and wondered if it was the body of a dancer.

Leah had filled out a little over the past couple of years. At five foot four, she weighed just one hundred pounds. She was sure she hadn't gotten too fat or too curvy or too tall. Her long legs were strong but shapely and not a muscle bulged anywhere. Her face was pretty in a rosy-cheeked, all-American sort of way: she had uncommonly large and round blue eyes and her fair skin tanned easily beneath the California sun. At least she wasn't the kind of blonde who looked washed out on stage. No, she thought objectively, she *looked* good enough to be a dancer.

"Stephenson! Are you going to stand there admiring yourself all day?" Miss Greene's voice was harsh and Leah jumped. Amy Moraldo and Patty Gonzalez started giggling. Leah blushed, then drew herself up very tall and pretended to ignore them. She stepped into her accustomed position at the head of the class. She sensed Chrissy falling into place behind her. "What are we doing?" Leah whispered through clenched teeth without turning around. She hadn't been paying attention. She had no idea what step was next.

"Four chaînés, four piqués," Chrissy prompted in a whisper. "Or maybe it was the other way around," she said uncertainly.

Leah nodded. She could figure it out. As the tinny strains of Tchaikovsky crackled out of the small tape recorder on the piano, she pointed her right foot in preparation. Just hearing *Swan Lake* did something to Leah. This might be the last moment of the last ballet class she'd ever take, and though she was aching to shout and scream and cry, she was determined to make this last dance her best. She wanted to show Miss Greene just how good she really was. *She'll be sorry,* Leah thought, taking several quick gulps of hot dry air and stifling the urge to cry. Piqué and chaîné turns were something she was very good at. She forced everything out of her mind and abandoned herself to the fiery rhythm of the music.

She waited two measures, then sprang strongly onto her right toe. She spun around quickly like a top: one, two, three, four times. In spite of her mood, a joyous smile came to her lips as she sped across the floor. For a moment Leah forgot about crying and Miss Greene, and the dreadful interview looming ahead, and just danced. With every step Leah took she felt more buoyant, as if she were made of light and air, not sweaty flesh and blood.

*   *   *

Ten minutes later Leah walked into the office and wanted to die on the spot. Miss Greene stood in the corner of the cramped, cluttered room with her back to Leah. But Leah didn't have to see her teacher's face to know this wasn't going to be a friendly rap session. The ex-ballerina's body language gave her away: her long back was tense, her shoulders hunched up. The way she was standing spoke louder than any words: whatever Hannah Greene had to say to Leah, it was bad news.

Leah rested one hand on the back of a chair, and whispered, "Miss Greene? I'm here." Her voice was almost swallowed up by the drone of an ancient air conditioner.

"Sit down." Without bothering to turn around, Hannah Greene gestured to the chair. She shifted a pile of records from one side of the desk to the other.

Leah obediently sank down into the roomy leather chair. Out of habit she tugged on her leg warmers and draped a sweater over her shoulders.

Sitting in air-conditioning after such an intense workout was bad for her muscles. Leah wondered vaguely why she still cared. Behind her the high, childish voices of the eight- and nine-year-olds filled the studio. Beginner class was about to start. Leah shifted restlessly in her seat. Inwardly she pleaded for her teacher to be quick and get the whole awful mess over with. To get her attention, Leah cleared her throat.

Miss Greene walked behind Leah and closed

the office door, abruptly shutting out the warmth and the sound of the children coming from the sunny studio. The tiny office seemed very dim by comparison, and icy cold. Leah pulled her sweater more tightly around her shoulders, and knotted the sleeves together in front, glad to have something to do with her hands.

Pushing aside a half-sewn red tutu, Hannah Greene finally turned around. She perched herself on the edge of the desk and picked up a container of cold coffee. She took a sip before looking directly at Leah. When she finally met Leah's frightened glance, her dark eyes softened.

After what seemed like forever she finally spoke up.

"Remember my friend Carmen Martinez and her partner Lou Evans?"

Leah nodded. "You mean the two Bay Area Ballet soloists who came to our recital last May?" she asked in a puzzled voice.

"Yes." Miss Greene took a deep breath. She looked down at her long slender hands and twirled around the narrow gold wedding band she wore on her left ring finger. She gnawed her lip and seemed lost in thought. Leah felt as if she were about to burst. Why didn't Miss Greene just come out and tell her to quit dancing? She'd rather hear the bad news all at once than have her teacher beat around the bush like this. She clutched the arms of her chair very tightly and had just mustered up the courage to say that, when Miss Greene continued. "Yes, they came to our recital and they liked it very much." She stood up and tugged down the back of the short black ballet skirt she wore for teaching. She walked over to the narrow window that looked out over the dirty backyard and peered through the cracked pane. After an excruciating moment, she turned around. Her arms were folded across her chest. Though she was smiling, she still looked sad.

"They were very impressed with the concert. Particularly with you, Leah."

"They were?" Leah gulped. For a moment she actually felt dizzy with relief. A faint ray of hope stirred inside her.

Miss Greene reached up over the window and flicked off the air conditioner. The room settled into silence. "It's too cold in here," she said absently, pulling a black shawl off the coat rack. She shrugged it around her narrow shoulders and went on.

"The point is, I invited them to the concert to get a strong second opinion—about you and your future. I had thought of waiting until January for this, but they were impressed enough to suggest that you go up to audition for entrance to the San Francisco Ballet Academy this fall."

"Audition?" Leah repeated incredulously. "You mean—you—they—think I could get into the Academy? This fall?" Her hands started shaking. She clasped them together and willed her heart to stop pounding. A second ago she had been sure her dream of being a dancer was dashed, over before she'd even gotten a chance to prove herself. Now she was about to be given the opportunity to try out for one of the top schools in the country, a school whose graduates almost always moved on into other respected ballet companies, if not the Bay Area Ballet itself. Leah suddenly didn't know if she was going to burst into laughter or tears.

"I think you stand a good chance of getting into the school. So does Carmen. They usually take only ten new girls at a time, but this year they have room for fifteen."

"Out of how many?" Leah asked.

"Over a hundred," Miss Greene replied.

Leah's eyes grew big. "A hundred?" she repeated in astonishment. "Oh, Miss Greene," she said, shaking her head back and forth. "Why would anyone pick me out of a hundred other girls?"

"Because you're gifted," Miss Greene responded instantly.

Leah blushed, feeling awkward in the face of such a direct compliment. Until this summer Miss Greene had always treated her as if she were special, but she had never said as much before. Leah felt incredibly happy and very proud.

Miss Greene continued, a warning note in her voice. "But as we all know, being gifted isn't always enough." After a pause she asked, "So, do you want to go ahead with it?"

Leah stared at her teacher in disbelief. "Do I *want* to audition?" She started to laugh. "Are you kidding?" She sprang to her feet and threw her arms around her teacher's neck. "Oh, Miss Greene, I want to audition and go to that school more than anything in the world."

Hannah returned her hug warmly, then pushed

her away, holding her at arm's length. Her own eyes filled as she said, "You've grown so much over the past few months. It's hard for me to believe you were once one of those babies out there." She gestured with her head toward the studio. "You are beginning to look like a real ballerina, Leah." She gazed at Leah a long moment. "I hate to lose you," she said wistfully, "but I'm afraid if you're to seriously consider a dance career, it's time for you to move on. I've taught you all I can here."

Hannah gave her head an annoyed shake. "Listen to me," the tight-lipped teacher said, suddenly embarrassed by her display of emotion. She dropped her hands from Leah's shoulders and continued brusquely. "Well, you'll have little enough to hug me about between now and next weekend. You're not going to love me once we start work on your audition program."

"Next weekend!" Leah shrieked. Her hands flew up to her head and she shook it back and forth trying to make the words she just heard go away. "You can't mean that. The audition isn't next weekend."

Miss Greene nodded. "It is. School starts in two weeks. The Ballet Academy operates on the usual school year schedule. If you get in, you'll have a couple of days to come back here and pack your clothes before going back to begin classes."

"But—" Leah paced over to the window and back again. She looked at Miss Greene with wide and frightened eyes. "I—I'm not ready. I mean, what do I have to do to audition?" she asked, sitting in the chair with a defeated thump.

"Take a class, then do a variation. That's all." Miss Greene struggled to keep a smile off her face. "You're ready for the class. I've been giving you the same level class you'll take from Madame Preston for the audition. And you can do the same variation from *Sleeping Beauty* you did at the recital."

Leah stared at her teacher and slowly a look of understanding crossed her face. "That's why you yelled at me all summer, isn't it? You were trying to get me ready for this." Leah suddenly felt awful for all the terrible things she had thought about Miss Greene, when all along her beloved teacher had only been trying to help her, prepare her for the future of her dreams. "I thought you were going to tell me I shouldn't dance anymore."

A pained expression crossed the teacher's high-cheekboned face. "I'm sorry I gave you that idea," she said. "I knew I was upsetting you, that I was pushing you very, very hard. It must have seemed unfair at times...."

Leah shifted uncomfortably as her teacher went on.

"But I had to see exactly how far you could come in a couple of short months. To see if you were really ready—technically and psychologically."

"But Annie was ready a whole year before me!" Leah burst out, then instantly wanted to take back her words. It sounded so petty, so silly, envying Annie, now that her own chance had come.

"Annie's different from you. She's the perfect type of dancer for the New York City Ballet, a real Balanchine dancer if I've ever seen one. But she's not as classical, as—" Miss Greene broke off and resumed in a sterner tone. "Annie is none of your business right now. No other dancer is. Do you hear me? All you have to pay attention to this next week is your own dancing. And when you get to those auditions, I want you to remember that. No one, nothing else will exist for you. No matter what happens."

Leah had never heard Miss Greene sound so fierce before. She nodded in agreement even though she wasn't sure she understood.

Miss Greene sighed again and began gathering some papers off her desk. "But I'm sorry if I undermined your confidence." She sounded worried. "I just want you to realize that the Academy is a very competitive place. If you do get in, this summer's classes are going to seem like child's play. I'm not half as demanding as Alicia Preston." Miss Greene gripped Leah's shoulder firmly and said in a clear no-nonsense voice, "But I never meant to have you doubt your ability to dance. You *are* a born dancer, Leah. And no matter what happens to you, never, ever doubt that one minute."

Her hand dropped from Leah's shoulder, and she glanced over at the wall. Leah followed her gaze. Her eyes rested on the framed photo of Miss Greene dancing the Bluebird with a famous male dancer. The picture was over twenty years old now, and Hannah Greene had left American Ballet

Theatre shortly after the photo was taken. An injury, followed by the desire to have children, had shortened her promising career. Leah had always wondered if Miss Greene regretted her decision to marry, have a family, and move to this dry, dusty California town, where her husband owned a prosperous artichoke farm. Teaching local kids ballet, tap, and drama seemed a far cry from dancing on the stage at New York's Metropolitan Opera House. It was a decision Leah knew in her heart she would never have made.

Miss Greene cleared her throat and continued. "The dance world is a very difficult one. Talent counts for a lot. Don't get me wrong. But at your audition there will be plenty of girls just as good as you. I think you'll make it, but you may not."

Leah's high forehead creased in a frown. The possibility of not getting in was too awful to think about.

"But if you do make the Academy, and graduate, you'll be lucky if you get into the corps of a regional company. And luckier still if you ever get to dance a solo role, let alone a lead."

Leah's face fell. The teacher reached out and affectionately tucked a stray wisp of blond hair behind Leah's ear. "But listen to me, Leah. Even dancing in a corps in a drafty school auditorium in the middle of Alaska is worth everything. It's the chance to perform and share your gift with people who love the beauty of the dance. So you see, if you don't believe it is worth it, then you should stop dancing now."

"Nothing could make me stop dancing now!" Leah responded vehemently.

Miss Greene smiled. "I know, Leah." She checked her watch. "Well, you may not be willing to stop dancing, but I have to get those kids out there started." She grabbed a tape from her desk, and added, "So we start tomorrow. I want to see you here at ten A.M. We'll work out a detailed schedule of rehearsals then, but be prepared to work into the evening at least a couple of nights. I want you to talk to your mother tonight and get her okay. Here are the particulars about the school." She handed Leah a catalog and a batch of forms.

"Oh, she'll say okay," Leah declared, knowing nothing in the world could keep her from the audition.

Chapter 2

"It's a boarding school?" Chrissy jerked with surprise and the top scoop of her ice cream cone teetered dangerously. She poked it securely back in place, licked her finger, then wiped her hand on the bright green sod surrounding Sneaky Pete's parking lot. On a far corner of the lawn the sprinklers made a slow swooshing noise, and drops of water fell to the ground glistening like jewels in the afternoon sun. Chrissy and Leah had headed directly from the dance class to San Lorenzo's popular hangout to celebrate Leah's big news.

Leah rolled her eyes at Chrissy's question. "Dumb, Morely. You're really dumb!" Leah paused to lick the edge of her frozen fruit bar, then let out a patient sigh. Sometimes her best friend's ignorance of dance matters was astounding. "For someone who's been studying ballet almost as long as I have, you don't know a thing.

"Tell my mother that!" Chrissy groaned, brushing crumbs from her cone off her white shorts. "Maybe she'll finally let me stop dancing. I've been studying nearly eight years, just like you, and I'm still not graceful. And I still hate ballet with a passion. Give me dogs, horses, cats, cows, the great outdoors," she said with an emphatic toss of her red braid. "I'm just not the indoor, cultured type. You know that. The problem is my mother doesn't."

Leah tilted back her head and laughed. The sun was bright in her eyes and she pulled down the sunglasses perched on top of her head and looked at her old friend with affection. "I'm really going to miss you, Chrissy!" she blurted out. She and Chrissy had been best friends since they were in first grade and had walked home together every day after school. Sometimes Leah was amazed they were still friends because they were so incredibly different. Chrissy was large-boned and clumsy. She wore thick glasses and was very knowledgeable about snakes, lizards, turtles, and other assorted wildlife. She was also a straight-A student. Leah wasn't any of those things and had always been glad to have Chrissy around to help her with her homework and explain exactly what made grass green and what caused rain. Leah helped Chrissy, too, with her dance classes and art projects and all the things Chrissy never had a knack for.

Leah could barely remember a time in her life when Chrissy hadn't been around to confide in. Chrissy was the one person who knew how awful Leah had felt when Annie had been chosen to audition two years ago and she hadn't. That's why Leah wished Chrissy looked a little more excited about her news. She leaned back on one arm and repeated thoughtfully, "Yes, I really am going to miss you."

"Oh, you'll be too busy dancing and becoming a star to remember your old friends," Chrissy said with an exaggerated sniff. "I can see the headlines in the San Lorenzo *Banner* now— HOMETOWN GIRL MAKES GOOD: DEBUTS WITH BARYSHNIKOV AT WAR MEMORIAL OPERA HOUSE."

Leah tossed a handful of grass at Chrissy. "Don't be such a jerk! Things like that don't happen in real life," she chided, but her heart skipped a beat. Could something so wild and wonderful actually happen to her in the not-too-distant future?

Chrissy tossed some of the grass back at Leah and shrugged. "Well, even if you don't run off and become an overnight dance phenomenon, I know how things are in boarding school." Chrissy kicked off her sandals and wriggled her pale toes in the grass. She stared sullenly at her feet and continued. "Everyone gets really tight with each other. You'll have a million new friends in a week. Just you watch. You'll forget all about your poor buddies back home in no time."

Leah knit her brow and stared out across the highway into the horizon. The fog was rolling in from the coast and the sky over the western hills was pale and hazy. "I'm not going to forget my friends," Leah stated emphatically. "Besides, it's not exactly a boarding school. We don't live on the grounds of the place. Academy students are placed with host families or in approved boarding houses."

Chrissy sat up straight and looked right into Leah's eyes. "You know what this all means, don't you?" she said in an ominous tone.

Leah shook her head, not quite sure she wanted to hear Chrissy's revelation.

"You're really leaving San Lorenzo." Chrissy paused for effect. She twirled one loose strand of red hair around her finger and continued slowly, emphasizing every word. "You are going to leave and never come back again."

"Come off it!" Leah dismissed Chrissy's prediction with a wave of her hand. "I haven't even gotten into the school yet. Don't forget, I've got to go up against a hundred other girls in an audition."

Chrissy laughed off Leah's fears. "You'll get in. You're the best student Miss Greene has ever had. And don't start talking about Annie Mac-Phearson." Chrissy cut off Leah's protest before Leah had a chance to open her mouth. "She didn't hold a candle to you and she got into a school. So you will too. But the point is, you're going to go to San Francisco, study there a couple of years, try out for a company, and be whisked away to who knows where. New York, Montreal, maybe even London or Paris. After this week I'll never see you again," Chrissy concluded in a tragic voice. She sighed, and flopped over on her stomach and stared forlornly at the ground.

Leah was speechless. So far Chrissy's reaction to her news hadn't been at all what she'd expected. Chrissy was supposed to be happy for her and here she was looking positively glum.

"Chrissy," Leah said, "I get the impression you

don't think my going to the Academy is such a great thing."

Chrissy gulped. "Oh, I do, I do. I mean, it's great." She paused, then added dramatically, "For you! But what about me? What about high school? Leaving San Lorenzo means we won't be in high school together."

"You? High school?" Leah started to laugh, but the deepening gloom on Chrissy's face stopped her and made her feel uncomfortable. Leah hopped to her feet and aimed the remains of her fruit bar toward the trash can. It fell woefully short. She jogged over to pick it up and toss it in. She quickly counted to ten before heading back to Chrissy. Sometimes her best friend was really exasperating. Leah hoisted the straps of her purple overalls back up on her shoulders and looked down at Chrissy.

"I don't see what my going to San Francisco has to do with you," she said, stuffing her hands into her pockets and rocking back and forth on her heels. If getting into a school connected with a major company was the first step on the ladder to success, nothing else should matter. This was the best thing that had ever happened to Leah, and Chrissy didn't seem to be the least bit excited for her. If something equally good had happened to Chrissy, Leah was certain she'd be overjoyed.

"I said I was going to miss you. And no matter what, we'll still be best friends," Leah asserted testily. "Why should the school I go to change that?"

Chrissy crossed her legs in an awkward lotus position and propped her chin on her hands. She stared at Leah skeptically for a minute. "I guess I was really looking forward to going to San Lorenzo High together. You know, the dances, the ball games, the parties. Meeting guys, all that normal everyday high school stuff."

Leah didn't know how to respond. Of course going off to the San Francisco Ballet Academy wasn't something every high school kid would do. But Leah wasn't every high school kid. She was a dancer and all she had ever wanted was to dance. When she danced she felt as if she were part of something bigger than herself, something very special that had existed for a long, long time. Just hearing the opening strains of any of the famous classical ballet pas de deux sent chills down her spine. Someday she'd be standing backstage in the wings listening to the overture, nervous, frightened, waiting for the curtain to rise and the ballet to begin. That was the world Leah dreamed of. If she could someday dance in *Sleeping Beauty*— even in the corps—missing out on normal high school life would be worth it.

But Chrissy didn't seem to understand that. No one Leah knew in San Lorenzo did, except Miss Greene, and Miss Greene was sending her away to the world where she belonged.

Leah looked at Chrissy and suddenly felt let down. "I didn't think being best friends meant we had a contract to go to school together," she said irritably. "We could have been assigned to different school districts. Everyone two blocks south of us is going to Gilroy Central High." She stopped and kicked her pink Reeboks against the trunk of a low sprawling oak tree. She reached up and dangled from one of its dark branches. "Friendship has to survive lots of ups and downs," she said more to herself than to Chrissy.

Chrissy looked at her coldly and said, "I'm not sure you know anything about being friends, Leah."

Leah let go of the branch and dropped to the ground.

"What are you talking about?"

Chrissy shrugged and began gathering up her things. "I think all you care about is dancing. No, not just dancing—*your* dancing."

"I don't believe you, Chrissy. Just because I'm not going to go to the same high school as you, you're telling me I'm self-centered, that I don't know how to be a friend. Well, I've always wanted to dance. You know that. I don't know why my going away should make me any less of a friend." She had to control herself to keep from shouting. How could her best friend in the world not understand that she was being given the chance of a lifetime? She couldn't stick around just so they could experience high school together.

Chrissy was right. All that mattered *was* her dancing. She looked at her friend, and wondered if she could ever understand that.

"Well, dancing isn't the only thing in the world, you know," Chrissy went on. "People are important too. People—like your friends, like *me*." She thumped her chest for emphasis.

"I know that." Leah paced over to the curb and

back again. She was beginning to wish she didn't have to wait for Chrissy's mother to give them a ride home.

"But you act like all that matters is your dancing." Chrissy pursued the argument. "You've always been like that, I guess," she added sadly. "I just never realized it bothered me until now." Chrissy looked from Leah in the parking lot to Sneaky Pete's takeout stand. She let out a loud sigh and said in a shrill voice, "What if you don't get in, Leah? What are you going to do then? Have you thought about that? What if you don't make it as a dancer, what happens next? What if you come back here after a year or two, and have no friends left?"

"I thought you said you believed in me," Leah said with a gasp.

"I do. I believe in you as a dancer." Chrissy shook her head in disgust. "But I'm not sure I believe in you as a friend anymore."

"Just because I'm going away to school?" Leah cried. She picked up her dance bag and slung it over her shoulder. Her voice trembled as she went on. "I know what's wrong with you, Chrissy. You're jealous," Leah accused suddenly. "I bet you—and half the other kids I know—would give their right arm to have a chance to go off and make a dream come true the way I do." Leah's voice rose a decibel with every word. Slowly a thought took shape in her mind. "You know what else?" she said in a low voice, and tapped Chrissy's shoulder with her finger.

Chrissy took a couple of steps backward, out of arm's reach.

"I think," Leah fumed, her eyes flashing fire, "that you wish you were half the dancer I am, that you wish you were in my shoes right now. Maybe I'll really get the chance to dance with some guy as great as Baryshnikov someday. All you can do is dream about it." Leah planted her hands on her hips and stared at her friend. Chrissy shrank back farther. "And you say I'm the one who's not a good friend. A good friend cheers her friend on when something good happens."

"That's not fair!" Chrissy cried, shocked at Leah's outburst. Her usually pale face was beet-red now, and her eyes brimmed with tears. "That's just not fair. But if that's how you feel about it, then I guess this is one friendship I'm glad is over."

The honk of a horn cut Chrissy off.

With her head held high Leah marched toward the Morleys' rusty station wagon. As she approached the car she quickly rubbed her arm across her face, wiping away the tears that were beginning to spill out of her eyes. She put on what Miss Greene had always called her best ballerina smile. "Hi, Mrs. Morley. I really appreciate the ride," she said, climbing in the back seat. She pushed down the door lock with an emphatic gesture as Chrissy hurried up behind her.

Chrissy flung open the front door and slipped in beside her mother. She pulled off her glasses and cleaned them on the front of her T-shirt, never once turning around to look at her friend.

Chapter 3

The night wind had picked up and the blue curtains fluttered out from the wide open window of Leah's ground floor bedroom. She knelt on the floor in front of her dresser sobbing over her fight with Chrissy. They had fought lots before, but not like this. Leah was half listening for the phone to ring, but she knew it wouldn't. Chrissy never made up first. She was too stubborn. and Leah was still too angry to call Chrissy herself and say she was sorry. Anyway, she wasn't sorry. Chrissy had betrayed her. She had pretended all along she had believed in Leah's dream. Now it turned out she thought Leah's dreams were just that, dreams that disappeared the minute you woke up—or grew up. Leah wasn't sure she could forgive her for that.

Sniffing back her tears, she energetically began to sort out her tights and leotards into three different piles: too far gone to be mended, mendable, good enough to bring to San Francisco for the audition. The audition pile was woefully small. For a moment she envied the other girls she knew, working summer jobs at the nearby Mission Canyon Mall. She was too busy dancing to ever have the time to earn her own spending money. Asking her mother for unnecessary dance gear right now seemed wrong. If she ended up actually going to SFBA, her tuition was going to be high, and although her mother could probably afford to send her, Leah knew she'd quietly cut some corners to do so. Of course her mother didn't even know about the audition yet.

Leah sat back on her heels and squinted out the window into the dark. She listened to the chirping of what sounded like thousands of crickets and smiled at the sound of Pavlova, the family dog, snuffling her way through some leaves in the front yard. Her mother's car was nowhere in sight. Leah glanced at the big blue plastic clock on her wall: nine-fifteen. The message on the answering machine had said her mother wouldn't be home from work until close to ten. Leah curled her bare toes in the thick blue-and-purple shag rug and inhaled sharply. The dry scent of eucalyptus and oranges from the yard filled her lungs. She closed her eyes and lifted her hair off the nape of her neck. She was wearing it down and it fell thick and straight almost to her waist. A cool breeze floated over her shoulders. A sudden pang of homesickness swept over her. What was wrong with her? She hadn't even left home yet, but she couldn't help thinking she was going to feel very alone without Chrissy, without Miss Greene, without her mom.

She'd been to San Francisco a couple of times

on school trips and liked it. But it was always foggy, and the air there was damp and smelled of the sea, more like down by Carmel or Monterey. Here in the inland valley everything was clear and dry. Leah had never lived anywhere else and she loved it. You could see for miles, and summer nights, no matter how hot the days, the temperature dropped until it was almost cold. The air was so pure the stars barely twinkled and they seemed so close Leah often felt like she could reach up and touch them. When she was a little girl she'd lie in her bed and look out her window at the swirling stars and fall asleep dreaming they were dancers wearing sparkly tutus, and she was dancing with them.

Pavlova suddenly let out an enormous woof. Leah sprang to her feet. A moment later headlights beamed down the long driveway and against her wall. "Mom! You're home!" Leah cried, tearing down the hall and out the kitchen door barefoot onto the grass. "Down Pavlova! Down girl!" she ordered as the huge pale mastiff made a beeline for her across the lawn. The big dog ran excited circles around Leah, then raced back to the driveway jumping and whining for glee as Bridget Stephenson slammed the door to the Subaru and walked slowly toward the house, one arm full of groceries, the other holding the straw carryall that served as her briefcase.

Leah held open the door and her mother entered the kitchen. She turned around and faced her daughter. The warm welcoming smile on her face turned to a frown of concern. "Leah, dear, you've been crying." She reached up to touch Leah's tearstained cheek. "What happened?"

Leah stepped back, confused. She had forgotten to wash off her face. "Nothing," she stated, suddenly feeling embarrassed about Chrissy. But her news was too big to think of Chrissy very long. Her mouth quickly widened into a huge smile. "Oh, Mom! *Everything!* Everything's happened!" She gleefully bit her lip, took the groceries from her mother's arms, and set the brown bag on the counter. She reached for her mother's hand and pulled her gently toward the family room that opened out from the brightly decorated kitchen.

"What's going on?" Mrs. Stephenson pretended to protest. She started laughing and her laughter filled the quiet house like music. *"Leah!"* she cried as her daughter whisked a sleepy kitten off the sofa and pushed her mother down into the soft cushions.

"Misha! You're supposed to sleep in the basket, not on the sofa." Leah gently scolded the little striped orange cat and deposited him on the rug.

"Leah, you'd better tell me what this is all about." Mrs. Stephenson eyed her daughter suspiciously.

Leah ignored her mother's comment and headed for the kitchen. "Are you tired? Do you want some tea?"

"No." Bridget Stephenson folded her hands firmly in her lap and studied Leah carefully. She was as dark as Leah was fair. Leah had inherited her father's coloring, but she had her mother's small slender build, delicate features, and beautifully sculpted face. "Are you going to let me in on your secret now?" Mrs. Stephenson asked before Leah could leave the room.

Leah turned around in the doorway and shifted from one foot to the other, trying to figure out how to begin. "I—well, in class today—oh, Mom," she finally cried, sinking to the floor at her mother's feet. She grabbed her mother's hands and looked up into her face with shining eyes. "I'm going to San Francisco to audition for the San Francisco Ballet Academy. Miss Greene's going to send me. She says I have a good chance of getting in." Leah kept her eyes on her mother's the whole time she spoke and strung her words together quickly. When she paused, the expression on her mother's face made her heart stop.

"Mom?" Leah said in a frightened voice. Still holding her hands, she got up and plopped down next to her on the sofa. Bridget Stephenson sat still as a stone. The color had drained from her face and her eyes were closed.

Finally she patted Leah's hand and said in a quiet, tired voice. "I think I'll have that tea now."

Leah got up slowly, afraid to say a word. On the way to the kitchen she repeated over and over like a prayer in her head, "Please let her say yes. Please let her say I can go." Only after she poured the tea did she realize she had used the lumpy brown glazed mug Chrissy had made and given her mom for Christmas. And then she realized that she hadn't *asked* her mother a thing. She had just *told* her she was going to San Francisco.

When she carried the steamy mug of tea back into the family room, her mother looked normal again. She was holding Misha on her lap and stroking him. Leah could hear the cat purring. "Why don't we start at the beginning," Mrs. Stephenson said with a brave smile. "What is this about going up to San Francisco—how, where, when? You know, all those unimportant details."

Leah relaxed a little. Her mother sounded more like her efficient business self. She pulled up the old rocking chair and curled her legs beneath her. She tugged her blue cotton nightgown over her toes and told her mother about her talk with Miss Greene and what she had learned about the school, ending with "and Miss Greene told me that if I want to dance professionally, I have to go now, to someplace bigger than San Lorenzo. I guess this is my big chance." Leah's voice dropped very low. For a moment the only sound in the room was the creak of Leah's rocking chair. Misha gave a tiny mew and awkwardly leaped from her mother's lap to Leah's.

"She's right," Mrs. Stephenson said, her voice sounding more like a sigh. She got up and carried her mug of tea to the window. Idly she picked the dead blossoms off a potted plant. She kept her back to Leah as she went on. "I feel you do have to move on. San Lorenzo's a pretty small town and you're too talented to stay here. I've always known that someday you would have to leave." She turned around and faced Leah, and a sad smile worked its way across her lips. "I just hadn't thought it would be so soon. I guess I didn't realize how you've grown. That in some ways you're already all grown up." Tears shone in her eyes.

Leah sprang to her feet and hurried to her mother's side. "Oh, Mom. I really love you." She threw her arms around her mother and hugged her tight. At that moment Leah only wished there were some way to make her dream come true without leaving her mother and San Lorenzo.

"I love you too, Leah. That's why this is so hard." Bridget stroked Leah's head and began to weep openly. Leah started crying too. For a few minutes they just held each other and rocked back and forth in front of the wide picture window. They hadn't cried together like this since Leah's father had died, and the memory made her cry harder now.

Finally her tears subsided. She swallowed the lump in her throat and looked up at her mother. "Can I go, then?"

Her mother smiled through her tears. "Of course, dear. It'll be lonely without you here, but I'll manage."

"I'm going to miss you, Mom."

"Yes, well, missing each other is the bad part of it, isn't it? But it can't be helped. I'm glad I don't have a daughter who's just dying to run away and leave home." Mrs. Stephenson sat down in a chair and looked around the room. She reached for a tissue and blew her nose. Her eyes rested on a framed photograph of Leah's dad.

"Your father would have wanted you to go, Leah. He believed you were born to do something

special with your life. I'm sure he'd send you off
to San Francisco quite happily if that's what it
takes for you to become a professional dancer."
Her voice was surprisingly steady. "We talked
about it once."

"But I was just a kid. I had just started dancing
seriously when Dad—died." Leah still found the
word hard to say.

"You were talented even then. Miss Greene told
us that if you worked hard, you could probably
have a very promising future in dance. Your father was proud of you for that. Like I am." Mrs.
Stephenson reached out and tousled Leah's tan-
gled hair. "But, Leah"—a cautious note entered
her mother's voice—"I hate to bring up unpleasant subjects."

"You mean the money," Leah jumped in. "There
are scholarships. I read the brochure."

Mrs. Stephenson laughed. "That's good news,
but I'm afraid my business has been doing a bit
too well to put you in the needy-student cate-
gory. The way things are going around here makes
me wonder what all these farmers did before
computers. I have more consulting than I can
tackle these days. No, money isn't the unpleasant
subject."

Leah's frowned, unable to fathom what was to
come next.

"What if you don't get in, Leah? Can you face
that? Are you prepared to fail?"

Leah's mouth fell open in surprise. "Mom, you
don't think I'll fail, do you?" Suddenly all her
newfound confidence vanished. Chrissy not believing in her was one thing, but her *mom* too?

Mrs. Stephenson let out another peal of laughter. "No, I don't think you are going to fail, but when you try out for something like this, it's like—" She searched for the right image. "It's like putting a bit of yourself out there for public inspection. And some of the public may not like what they see no matter how good it is."

Her mother's meaning began to dawn on Leah. "You mean, do I think I'm good enough no matter what anyone else thinks?" Leah asked. "And will I keep on dancing no matter what anyone says?"

Her mother nodded.

Leah sat very still and studied her hands. When she finally looked up at her mother, she admitted with a sigh, "I don't know, Mom. I guess I'll find out about that, but right now I don't think anything in the world can keep me from dancing. Nothing!" she concluded with a force that surprised her.

"I don't think so either," her mother stated firmly. "And I'm glad you feel that way, because to pursue a career in dance you'll have to give up a lot: the fun of high school life, the dances, the parties, time with your friends."

"I never just hang out with my friends anyway," Leah remonstrated hotly. "And I *hate* doing nothing!" she continued, giving a distasteful little shiver. Sitting still too long, reading or talking, had always driven her crazy. It was her passion for movement that had led her parents to start her at pre-dance at a community center when she was just four. "If I can dance someday with a company, even in the corps," Leah declared passionately, "then whatever I'm missing now will be worth it."

That night Leah crept into bed too exhausted to sleep. Her legs ached from class, she had a blister on her right toe. Her mind was racing and she had a strange hollow feeling in the pit of her stomach. Somehow, alone in the dark, looking up at the stars as she lay in her bed, Leah didn't feel as sure and confident of her future as she had earlier in the day. What if she didn't make it past the first cut in the audition? She would be so humiliated. She'd be letting other people down. Miss Greene, of course, and her mother. Leah choked up at the thought of her mother. As far back as Leah could remember, her mom had encouraged her to dance. But not in the same way that Annie MacPhearson's mom had encouraged her, or like the mothers of other less talented kids who ended up at Hannah Greene's School of Dance and Theater Arts.

Leah's mom had never pushed her. In fact, she always urged Leah to slow down, not to work so hard, to go out with friends.

But Leah had always wanted only to dance, and her mother had helped her every step of the way. Now, with any luck at all, she'd be moving away to San Francisco and leaving her. She knew her mom would do just fine. She had lots of friends, and had even begun dating a bit recently. But Leah's bond with her mother was strong, and Leah knew how much she was going to miss her mother's strong, reliable presence.

What would life be like without her mom? Without Chrissy's shoulder to cry on? Chrissy had been so sure Leah would have a whole new group of friends within a week. Leah doubted that. Besides, no one would be an old, true-blue friend like Chrissy. She'd be heading into a brand-new life, full of new people, and the thought didn't excite her. It scared her. She'd never lived with other girls before. She had never even lived with a brother or sister. Suddenly, except for the prospect of dancing morning, noon, and night, the future didn't look so bright at all. Tears built up behind Leah's eyes and she willed herself not to cry. Her mother would hear her and worry, and besides, she had cried enough today.

She stared out the window and told herself she was the luckiest girl in the world. She repeated it over and over until she almost believed it.

She pushed the curtain aside with her hand and picked out the brightest, biggest star she could find in the sky, then did something she hadn't done since she was ten and she and Chrissy and Sue Anne Crewdson had camped out in the Morleys' backyard. She made a wish, praying with all her heart that her dream of being a real ballerina would someday come true, and make leaving home worth all this. Just to be certain, she picked out a second star, and made another fervent wish for something smaller and more immediate. "Please," she whispered into the dark, "let me get through that audition and just get the chance to study at SFBA."

Chapter 4

Thick morning fog hung over the valley, though just above the eastern horizon the sky shone gold above the fields. Within the hour the clouds would lift and it would be another clear hot September day in San Lorenzo, but Leah wouldn't be there to see it. She sat inside the nearly empty Greyhound bus, her head aching, her eyes red from crying all night. Now that leaving home had become a reality, Leah was tempted to run off the bus and fly into her mother's arms and forget about dancing. She was feeling like an uprooted tree. It was a terrible feeling, as if parts of her she never knew existed were stretching out and back behind her, hanging on to all the things she had once called home.

Leah hadn't thought it would hurt like this, and she knew Chrissy's not coming to see her off made it all worse. She hadn't told her mother about the fight with Chrissy, about how they hadn't seen each other once all week. But her mom had probably guessed: Chrissy not hanging around the house was pretty unusual.

Leah sat with her nose pressed against the window, trying to smile at her mother through the grit. The driver had made her climb on board early and closed the door behind her. Now he lingered outside People's Drugs talking to the dispatcher and sipping coffee out of a blue paper cup. Leah drummed her fingers anxiously against the vinyl back of the seat in front of her, thinking about Chrissy and how their friendship would never be mended. Leah had believed Chrissy had really wanted her to become a dancer; now she felt betrayed.

But the hurt went deeper than that. The more she thought of it, the more she realized some of what Chrissy had said had sounded like the truth, the kind of truth that scared Leah. Did she really care only about herself? Was devoting herself to dance selfish? Had she stopped caring about other people? Leah stared out the window at her mother. Leah had never noticed before how small she looked. Quickly she averted her eyes, wiping tears from her cheeks. Leaving San Lorenzo was turning out to be the hardest thing she'd ever done, and she wished she could just get it over with.

Her mother tapped on the window to get Leah's attention, then pointed to her wristwatch, miming something about the bus leaving soon. Right on cue the driver shrugged off his jacket and opened the bus door. Seconds later they pulled out, and Leah felt free to let her tears flow. She was crying a little because of Chrissy, because leaving without saying good-bye to Chrissy felt as if she were cutting off her childhood forever. But she was crying mostly because she was leaving home and her mother. She stifled a sob and rested her head against the window, watching her mother grow smaller until she was nothing but a tiny solitary figure on the deserted street. The bus turned off Main Street and onto the access road to Highway 101 and Leah let her head fill with all the good memories of San Lorenzo.

Two hours later Leah stood on the windy corner of Market and Hyde streets trying to decipher a San Francisco street map and still thinking of Chrissy. She only wished she had listened when her friend had tried to get her to join the Girl Scouts so she could learn to read maps. She nervously gnawed the inside of her lip, looked right, then left, trying to figure out which way was north. The San Francisco Ballet Academy lay in the north of the city, somewhere near the Golden Gate Bridge. Leah looked around hoping to catch a glimpse of the graceful suspension bridge, but all she could see were cars and buses and pedestrians making their way across the busy intersection. Her heart sank. This audition week was starting out just great. Leaving home without making up with her best friend, landing in a city she barely knew, too shy to ask directions. As far as she was concerned, SFBA might as well be a million miles away.

"Excuse me, but are you a dancer?" a sultry voice drawled from somewhere close behind Leah.

Leah whirled around and found herself looking into the inquisitive green eyes of a truly beautiful girl. Her thick auburn hair was pulled back into a high ponytail and her pale creamy complexion was flawless. Leah's hand automatically went to her own face and fingered a tiny blemish on her chin. "Uh, yes," she answered.

A merry laugh went up from another, shorter girl standing next to the redhead. Wild dark curls tumbled down to her shoulders, and a thick barrette did little to keep her hair back out of her eyes, which were a startling deep shade of blue. Leah liked her instantly.

"I told you so, Pamela," the short girl said, looking at Leah with frank admiration. "When I spotted you on the corner, with your hair in a bun, looking every inch the ballerina—holding a map—I figured you were yet one more victim for this year's SFBA auditions. We are too. We ran into each other on the airport bus."

Leah returned the girl's warm inviting smile and said, "My name's Leah Stephenson, and I am heading to the Academy, if I can find it, that is."

"My name's Kay Larkin. Katherine, if you want to be formal about it. No one calls me that, though it's a far more elegant stage name than Kay, don't you think?" She turned toward the redhead. "This is Pamela Hunter, she's from Atlanta. I'm from Pennsylvania, not far from Philadelphia. Neither of us have been here before. It's awfully cold for September," she added with a shiver, and snapped up her denim jacket.

Leah nodded agreement and tugged her purple sweatshirt down over her slim-cut white pants. "Would you believe this is the warmest month of the year here? At least the sun's out. Most days it's foggy."

"Like in *Dark Passage*?" Kay's eyes grew wide. "That's my favorite Bogart flick, and I read it was filmed not far from the school. I never thought all that fog was for real."

Pamela arched her finely penciled eyebrows and smiled tolerantly. In a bored, impatient voice she asked, "Where is this place anyway? I'm exhausted. I just want to get to my room, take a hot bath, and go to sleep. The flight was endless and I've never felt so stiff in all my life. I just can't believe we have to actually audition after all this traveling. I don't know how I'll ever get through it." She jutted out her foot and flexed it experimentally. She was wearing snug black ankle boots, but even through the smooth leather the strong arch of her foot was clearly visible.

I'll bet she's got no trouble on pointe! Leah thought enviously. She looked at Pamela more carefully. The redhead's luxurious sweater-jacket didn't conceal her trim dancer's body. Beneath her leather miniskirt, her shapely legs looked sturdy and strong. She was a curvy, compact type, not lithe like Leah. *Ten to one she has a great jump,* Leah thought. In fact, even without a jump her looks alone would probably get her into any of the major ballet companies in the country in a couple of years.

She turned to Kay. The dainty dark-haired girl was not the ideal height for a dancer, but she was perfectly proportioned. Even standing still she seemed to be a blur of movement and energy. She had enough suitcases with her for a month, and was juggling them around trying to find some way to carry them all at one time. Everything about her pointed to quickness and speed. She was obviously one of those sparkling allegro dancers Leah had always admired, the kind whose feet skimmed the stage like a hummingbird's wings. Next to Kay, five-foot-four Leah felt big and clumsy.

All at once Leah realized what she was thinking and blushed. Never in her life had she looked at other girls and sized them up as competition. Of course she hadn't had to, either. At the Hannah Greene School Leah had always been the star pupil; even Annie MacPhearson had expected Leah to share the best roles in the annual school show. Leah had seldom found herself fighting for top billing. But just five minutes talking to Pamela Hunter and Kay Larkin had shaken Leah's confidence. Even in their street clothes they seemed to be the best young dancers Leah had ever seen up close, and she couldn't help wonder if the judges would pick her over either of them.

Miss Greene had warned her about exactly how competitive things would get during audition week, and at the Academy itself if she actually got in. But she wasn't used to feeling competitive. She had never thought of herself as that kind of person. Leah frowned, wondering how many other things about herself she didn't know yet. She had a funny feeling that becoming a real dancer was going to mean more than learning how to dance.

"So now that we know we're all going to the same place, how do we get there?" she asked brightly, determined not to let competitive vibes get in the way of making two new friends. With any luck all three of them would get in to SFBA. She looked from Pamela to Kay and back to Pam again. Pamela seemed older, more sophisticated, as if she would know how to get around a city she'd never been to before.

"Cab!" Pam declared, shifting her Gucci dance bag from her right shoulder to her left.

Kay's blue eyes bulged. She stood on tiptoe and tapped Leah's map with her elbow. "According to this we can walk. It's only a mile or two, right up this way." She gestured with her chin.

"Walk?" Pam repeated scornfully as the wind gusted around the corner. She tossed her ponytail behind her shoulder and eyed Kay with obvious disdain. "Where I come from, dancers don't walk. Not if they can help it. It's bad for the knees."

Kay's mouth fell open. She ogled Pam in silence for a moment, then started to laugh. She dropped her suitcases to the sidewalk, where they landed with a thump. She doubled over, still laughing, until Leah finally joined in. When Kay finally recovered, she wiped the tears from her eyes. "I'm sorry, Pam. But I never heard anything like that before. Back home I walk a mile from my house just to get to the school bus stop. It's never hurt my legs. I guess our teachers have different theories about what dancers should and shouldn't do for exercise."

Kay sounded so cheerful and blasé, Leah was amazed. Pam's remark had a definite tart edge to it. She looked over at Pam. The redhead's lips curved down in a pouty frown and from the set of her chin Leah sensed Pam was on the verge of making a big thing about taking a cab. Leah wasn't in the mood to get into the middle of an argument between the two girls about transportation. She thought quickly. "Hey, it's still early," she began.

Pam arched her eyebrows and took a step toward the curb. Leah hurried on, not wanting to give her a chance to hail a cab. She didn't know the first thing about Pam or Kay, but she remembered that the SFBA brochure said half the students were on full scholarship. Pam's Gucci bag and expensive outfit suggested money wasn't one of her problems; but maybe Kay didn't have the extra cash to blow on cab fare.

"We can take a bus. Our suitcases are really too heavy to carry." Before Pam could protest, Leah picked up her own bags and, looking more confident than she felt, marched down Market Street toward Van Ness. Pam and Kay straggled behind in her wake. Leah kept up a constant stream of chatter and didn't let the other girls get a word in edgewise. As she hurried along, she hoped her hazy interpretation of the street map had been more or less correct.

A few minutes later she pointed triumphantly to a sign. "See!" she said. "There's a bus stop, going north on Van Ness. And I know the War Memorial Opera House where the company performs is right on Van Ness. I went there once to see *Nutcracker*. We'll pass it as we go by. Just think, if we luck out on this audition, we might get to dance there someday." Leah ushered the girls toward the curb as a city bus pulled up. "We can always ask the driver exactly where we get off for the school."

Chapter 5

"How quaint!" Pamela commented
twenty minutes later as the three girls stood in
front of the huge Victorian mansion that housed
the San Francisco Ballet Academy. From the way
she said it, Leah could tell that in Pamela Hunter's eyes quaintness rated about a zero on a scale
of one to ten.

But Leah wasn't paying any attention to Pam.
She stood spellbound in front of the school. Traf-
fic zoomed down the busy avenue behind her; a
stiff cold breeze whipped up from the bay just
below. But everything and everyone seemed to
recede into the background as she got her first
glimpse of the school she hoped would be her
home for the next three years. The drawing on
the cover of the Academy brochure only vaguely
resembled the building in front of her. It certainly
hadn't captured its charm. Leah had never seen
so many balconies, terraces, bay windows, and
turrets in a single structure. San Lorenzo boasted
flat one-story ranch houses, and some lovely old
mission-style buildings with pale adobe walls and

red tiled roofs. But nothing like this. Trumpet vines and morning glories festooned one side of the yellow painted building. A rose arbor in full bloom arched across the grass to the right of the porch. To the left of the house, overlooking the cliff leading down to the bay, there was a white wooden gazebo. Leah had never seen anything so perfect in all her life. The whole place looked like the setting for the kind of romance novel Leah loved.

She let out a happy sigh. She had come to SFBA only because she wanted to become a great ballerina. Now she had a second overpowering reason to succeed at next week's audition: she had fallen in love with the school itself at first sight. She'd give anything to be accepted here. The building and grounds were straight out of her dreams.

"I thought places like this were destroyed during that big old earthquake!" Kay said, suspiciously eyeing a crack in the cement walk that led up to a wrought iron front gate. "Isn't that San Andreas Fault somewhere nearby?" She looked nervously up and down the block.

Hearing Kay's fears broke Leah's spell. "You'll get used to earthquakes. They happen all the time around here, so slight you barely notice the tremor. But that—" she tapped the cracked pavement with the toe of her sneaker, "is definitely not a fault line." Her blue eyes glinted with mischief as she added, "At least not a dangerous one." She gave Kay an affectionate poke. Kay's frightened expression gave way to a sheepish giggle, and

Leah found herself hoping that both she and Kay would be accepted at the school. She was definitely someone Leah could be friends with.

"Well, I don't know about you two, but my poor little southern bones are freezing. Let's get inside and find out what we do next," Pamela suggested with a shiver. "I can't wait to see their modern facilities!" she added caustically.

Leah wasn't about to argue. She was cold too. They hurried down the path across the spacious front yard and up the broad front steps of the porch. Above the heavy knocker was a brass plaque:

SAN FRANCISCO BALLET ACADEMY

it said, and in smaller print just below

SCHOOL OF THE BAY AREA BALLET

Before she could knock, the door swung open and a dark-haired boy swept out. "Look what the wind blew in!" he called back over his shoulder to someone Leah couldn't see. His voice was haughty, and he looked disdainfully from Kay to Pamela to Leah, then smiled in a very superior way. "Auditionees, I presume." With that he gave an exaggerated bow and motioned them through the door. He straightened up and rudely pushed by Leah out onto the porch.

"James, close the door behind you please," a voice cried out from the dark foyer. But the boy didn't seem to hear.

His voice floated back toward Leah. "Good luck!" The way he said it sounded almost like a sneer.

Leah cringed. She turned on her heel and let the other girls go in first. "Same to you," she murmured under her breath, and watched him vault down the front steps and start down the path. She looked at the tall boy with obvious distaste, not that he was unpleasant to look at. His back was straight as an arrow. His oversized flannel shirt hung loose over his slim black jeans and a deep red sweater hung knotted by its sleeves around his neck. From his walk Leah could tell he was a dancer. He was definitely one of the best-looking boys Leah had ever seen, but also one of the rudest people she'd ever encountered. She entered the building wondering if all the guys in the school were as stuck up as he.

"Very cute!" Kay muttered under her breath as Leah caught up to her. "I wonder if he's trying out."

"Not now," Pam said. "Boys auditioned separately a couple of months ago. The ones who make it *all* get scholarships."

"Are you girls here to audition?" A kindly male voice spoke up from farther down the hall. Leah nodded and headed for the long table that filled the width of the spacious entranceway. Behind the table the hall ended with a large modern picture window that looked out over the back-yard. A couple of modern-looking stone buildings lined the edge of the property. One was clearly the bubble-topped swimming pool the school had proudly advertised in its fliers. The other had a sign saying ART STUDIO. Leah wondered how dancers ever found the time to swim, let alone paint or draw.

At the table sat a sandy-haired man who also looked like a dancer. He had small laugh lines around his mouth and his face was very kind.

He introduced himself with a laugh. "Patrick Hogan. And please call me Patrick. Mr. Hogan makes me feel much too old." Leah's eyes lit up with recognition. She had seen him dance the male lead in *Nutcracker* a few years ago. He was a principal dancer with the Bay Area company, but he looked different, smaller, and definitely more approachable offstage, without makeup and out of costume. She hadn't expected members of the company to be helping out with registration for auditions. "Why don't you put those bags down over there," he continued, motioning to an alcove beneath the broad-stepped spiral suitcase. "I'll have Raul put them in the school van. After someone shows you around and you get your schedules, he'll drive you right to your assigned boarding-houses and rooms. You're probably pretty wrecked from traveling and will want to sit back and relax the rest of the afternoon."

Within minutes he had located their pre-registration cards in one of several large boxes lined up on the desk. Leah was delighted to find herself assigned to the same boardinghouse as Kay and Pamela. Having familiar faces around tonight would help take her mind off being away from home, and whatever terrors loomed ahead on the audition front tomorrow. "Is Mrs. Hanson's boarding-house far from here?" she asked shyly.

Patrick shook his head. "You can walk back and forth from class. Most of our housing facilities are pretty close to the school. You save bus fare." He picked up a phone and dialed a number on the intercom. "You'll like Mrs. Hanson," he went on. "She's our director's sister. Though you'd never know it from looking—" He broke off and asked whoever answered the phone to come up to the front desk.

"This is Diana Chen," Patrick said as a young woman wearing a black leotard, navy blue sweater, pink tights, and raggedy gray leg warmers appeared out of the back hall. Leah's eyes widened. Diana Chen had been featured in last month's issue of *Foot Notes* as one of the top young ballerinas in the country. She had looked very remote and dreamy in the feature photo, not at all like someone who'd wear ballet slippers mended with duct tape. She was carrying a clipboard in one hand and a cup steaming with tea in the other.

Diana smiled warmly at the three girls. "Most of the other kids got here already, so by now my show-and-tell routine is beginning to sound old hat," she said. Her voice was light and musical and reminded Leah of the sound of bells. "Why don't you hang your jackets on the rack, and I'll give you the grand tour and tell you a little about the school and what you can expect over the next few days."

Kay groaned and sank in a mock faint against the tastefully papered wall. Diana gave her a sympathetic look. "Hey, it's not all that bad," she said, leading them up the stairs.

For the next half hour Leah felt as if she were on some kind of crazy roller-coaster ride. Diana's tour of the dance facilities left her breathless. There were several large airy studios with gleaming floors, shiny black grand pianos, and high modern windows looking out over the bay. Smaller rehearsal spaces and music rooms filled the third floor. The basement housed a sizable library of dance and music books, tapes, and videos. A whole modern wing, not visible from the street, was the site of the academic classrooms. Leah groaned when she saw algebraic equations scrawled on the green chalkboard. Without Chrissy around, algebra was going to be pretty tough.

Diana's tour ended in what the dancer affectionately called the school auditorium. It had formerly been the ballroom of the old mansion. The girls gathered around her on a sofa toward the back of the dark paneled room. "Tomorrow I suggest you all come to class," Diana said. "Some of the company is still away on vacation, but our fall work schedule is starting up this week. If you look at the envelopes Patrick gave you, you'll see your class assignment: Red Studio, Blue Studio, or Green Studio. We've tried to divide the auditioning students up so that there are professionals, current students, and some of you guys in each morning class."

"So the audition really starts tomorrow?" Pam asked pointedly, drumming her fingers on the arm of the sofa, her eyes darting around the room taking everything in.

Diana shook her head. "No," she said firmly.

"Morning class is just that—morning class. It will be a hard class for you, as it is geared toward those of us in the company already, but no one will be judging you at all. But on Tuesday you will be divided up in groups and every girl will have to take a class given by Madame Preston."

"We don't meet her until then?" Leah asked, disappointed. She had heard about Alicia Preston from Miss Greene. Looking over at the large framed photograph of the school's director hanging to the right of the double French doors, Leah felt a strong desire to meet her, although the prospect of being around such a famous teacher scared her half to death. Madame Preston was a stern-looking woman with steel-gray hair and elegant features. Leah imagined she must have been extremely beautiful when she was young.

"No. Not until then. She's the main judge at the audition and likes to keep an open mind about the students. Madame Preston's class is phase one of your test. About a third of your score will have to do with technique and proficiency at the barre and during your centre work. Part two, as I'm sure you know, is your solo variation. Your audition times will be posted on the call-board just inside the front door. Keep your eyes on that board: lots of notices will go up while you're here and you'd better read them all."

Diana glanced at her watch and stood up. "I've got a rehearsal right now. If you have any questions, I'll try to answer them quickly."

Leah didn't know about the other girls, but she was too overwhelmed to think of questions. Diana's outline of the audition procedure came as no surprise to her. Miss Greene had told her all about the class, and of course she had already rehearsed her variation so many times she was practically dancing it in her sleep. Still, actually sitting in the Academy auditorium and hearing the details in person made Leah's skin crawl. A wave of fear washed over her, and she managed to miss whatever question Pam had asked their guide. She took a couple of deep breaths and forced herself to listen to what Diana was saying.

"—plenty of practice time. You're required to attend class only in the morning. The rest of the time is more or less your own. You'll each have a couple of rehearsal sessions privately with the accompanist who will play during your solo audition. Sign-up sheets will be posted tomorrow, and I suggest you visit the call-board before the ten o'clock class and schedule your private rehearsals. Otherwise you might find yourself rehearsing at eight in the morning or well into the night."

Leah's head was spinning by the time she followed the other girls out the side entrance to the building and onto the small parking lot. The more she saw of the school the more determined she was to get in. But the more she heard about the audition, the more convinced she was she might not make it.

"I guess that's our ride," Kay said, pointing to a royal blue van parked in the corner. A trim, athletic-looking man with a thin dark mustache was loading their luggage into the back. He introduced himself as Raul. He looked so much like a dancer, Leah wondered if everyone who worked at the school was a member of the company. She was about to ask him, when he mentioned he was codirector of San Francisco's new experimental Teatro Hispanico, and exchanged work around the school for dance classes for himself and some of his fellow actors. From time to time he coached the male students in fencing, he told them.

"And now to Mrs. Hanson's," Raul said, opening the passenger doors so the girls could climb in. He had a pleasantly deep voice and spoke with a faint Spanish accent. "You're some of the lucky ones. She's got the best boardinghouse in town, and if good vibes help you get through auditions, you're off to a very promising start." He turned on the ignition and pulled the van out into the long circular drive that led out to MacDonald Way.

Chapter 6

The boardinghouse was not at all far from the Academy though it was in a decidedly shabbier neighborhood. Leah felt silly being chauffeured the half mile to the stucco-faced row house.

"This is the place, my friends," Raul announced, parking the van and jumping out. "Last one out's a dead swan," he joked. Only Kay laughed. Pam stood forlornly on the sidewalk looking at the narrow three-story building. "At least we're just staying here for a couple of nights."

"Right," Leah said, unable to mask her own disappointment. "It isn't as if we're going to live here." After the grandeur of the Academy itself, Mrs. Hanson's modest house was a real letdown.

Kay remained upbeat. "The flowers are pretty," she remarked, pointing to the window boxes filled with purple petunias and showy red geraniums. "And Raul said this is a lucky place to stay, didn't you?" She looked trustingly in his direction.

Raul returned Kay's warm smile. "You bet, little one! A very lucky place, because Madame Preston's sister is a very special woman. Good luck to you all," he added, waving good-bye and clattering down the stairs. "I've got to get back to the Academy for the next vanload."

Pam rang the doorbell. A moment later the door opened and a short round woman stepped out onto the small porch. Her face was a landscape of wrinkles and she looked as if she belonged in a fairy tale. Her waist bulged out comfortably where it should have gone in, and her cheeks were full and rosy. Leah had the strongest urge to hug her. Suddenly she believed Raul was right when he said staying here would bring them luck.

Leah met the woman's eyes and somehow knew instantly this was Madame Preston's sister. Her face lit up with a huge smile. "You must be Mrs. Hanson," she said, though the homey-looking person in front of her didn't resemble the photograph of the stern director of the Academy in the least.

The woman nodded. "Yes, I am. And you, I gather, are my first batch of girls for next week's auditions." She looked at each of them over in turn. Only then did Leah notice that Mrs. Hanson's eyes were the same penetrating gray that had peered at her from Madame Preston's photograph. Apparently Pam didn't notice the resemblance.

"You can't be Madame Preston's sister," she declared, sounding as if there had been some kind of terrible mistake.

To Leah's surprise, Mrs. Hanson laughed heartily. "Everyone says that. Alicia and I are definitely not as alike as two peas in a pod. That's why she dances and I see to her dancers."

She ushered the girls into the narrow front hall. Above the old-fashioned wainscoting, dainty ivory and blue flowered paper brightened the otherwise dim entranceway. A generous bouquet of fresh cut peonies burst from a vase on a narrow table against one wall. Farther down the hall wooden pegs driven into the molding served as a coat rack.

The hall widened just before reaching the front stairs. To the right, double French doors opened into a spacious old-fashioned living room. An old upright cluttered with open sheet music stood in the corner. There were plenty of overstuffed chairs and a couple of sofas, all threadbare, but comfortable and inviting. Beyond the living room Leah glimpsed an open door leading into what looked like a bedroom. It was flooded with light and Leah wondered if it would be hers.

The place was nothing like her mother's tastefully furnished modern house, but Leah felt perfectly at home. She crossed her fingers in her pockets and made a wish that if she did get into SFBA, somehow she'd end up living right here.

"Wow, something smells great!" Kay exclaimed, craning her neck to get a glimpse of the kitchen. The hearty aroma of something cooking wafted out of a door to the left of the stairs.

Mrs. Hanson stopped bustling in the hall closet and turned to smile at them over her shoulder. "And it isn't half as fattening as it smells." She chuckled. "I haven't been feeding dancers for twenty years without learning a thing or two."

Leah breathed a discreet sigh of relief. Mrs. Hanson's plump figure didn't exactly inspire confidence in her own ability to stay thin if she lived here, assuming she even passed the audition.

"Why don't you girls go upstairs and settle into your rooms. I'm sorry you won't get to meet the rest of the boarders. The house is fairly empty now. Most of the regular students are home for vacation and, of course, it's the start of a new semester. Some of the girls won't be back this year." She fished a pair of wire-framed reading glasses out of her pocket and settled them on her nose, then turned and rifled through a pile of index cards on the hall table.

"Let's see now. Which of you is Pamela?" Mrs. Hanson peered over the top of her glasses at the redhead. "You're in the back room on this floor. Right through the living room. And Kay?" She looked from Leah to Kay. Before Kay could even identify herself, Mrs. Hanson seemed to guess which one she was. "You're upstairs on the second floor, third door down the hall to the left. And Leah, you're on the third floor, the room at the top of the stairs. It's a bit of a climb, but it's worth it."

As the girls grabbed their bags and started toward the stairs, the doorbell rang again. "Batch two!" Mrs. Hanson announced happily. She peered at her cards and rattled off some names: "Katrina, Linda, and Sally. That should do it." Turning back to the girls, she suggested, "Now you go and get yourselves settled, take showers, and a little nap. We can get better acquainted over supper. That's at five o'clock today, since I bet not one of you had lunch. And you'll probably want to turn in early after all that traveling. You'll want to get some rest before things start hopping on Monday."

She tucked the index cards into her apron pocket and went to greet the newcomers.

Leah helped Kay cart her bags up the steps. On the landing Kay stopped to massage her arms. "I brought all this because if I do get in, I won't go home again before classes start. My mom will send a trunk with winter things later. Meanwhile—" Kay grinned, reshouldered her bag, and clunked noisily up to the second floor.

"It's probably smart to think positively," Leah observed as she put Kay's duffel bag down at the head of the stairs before continuing up to the next landing. "I bet everyone who tries out is very good." She looked at Kay, absolutely envying her tiny build. Still, something about the Pennsylvania girl prompted Leah to confide in her. With a nervous laugh she said, "It makes me wonder why anyone would pick me over someone else."

"Everyone feels like that when they get here," a heavily accented voice said.

Leah looked up. A girl stood in the doorway of a bedroom at the top of the stairs. She was taller than Leah and her black hair was pulled back tightly into a severe bun. Her lips were unusually full and she was wearing a deep red gloss. Her jet black stretch pants and turtleneck contrasted sharply with the brilliant decor of the bedroom behind her. Leah couldn't quite tell how old she was and wondered if she was there to audition, was already a student or a teacher at the Academy, or even a professional dancer. Leah seriously doubted she was from the Bay Area Ballet. She had a souvenir book from the company's spring season and had a great memory for faces. Even if the girl were in the last row of the corps, Leah would not have forgotten those huge almond-shaped dark eyes that gazed intently at her now.

She shifted uncomfortably under the girl's unwavering gaze. If she turned out to be another "auditionee" as James had called them, Leah felt she was in big trouble. How could she compete with a teenage dancer who looked as polished as that?

Kay grinned at the girl and said, "Hi, I'm Katherine Larkin. You can call me Kay. I'm here to audition."

The girl graciously bowed her head and her full lips turned up into a smile. "I'm already a student here. So you don't have to size me up as competition." She flashed a quick glance at Leah. Leah got the uncomfortable feeling the girl could read her thoughts. Turning back to Kay, the girl said, "You can call me Alex. That's short for Alexandra Sorokin."

Kay's eyes widened. "Sorokin. You are related to—" She broke off and slapped her hand to her forehead. "I don't believe this. Leah—" Kay excitedly grabbed Leah's arm and pointed at Alex. "She's the daughter of Olga and Dimitri Sorokin!"

Leah was impressed. The Sorokins had defected from the Soviet Union while on tour with the Kirov Ballet four years before. Their "leap to freedom" had been headline news for weeks. Leah studied Alex more carefully. She really did resemble her famous father, with the same high cheekbones and full mouth. At the time of the Sorokins' defection, Leah had followed the coverage on the TV news every day. The Sorokins had timed their defection to coincide with their dancer daughter's stint as an exchange student at a major Canadian ballet school. Eventually the family was reunited in Washington. It was hard to believe this was the twelve-year-old girl she had seen rushing from the steps of a plane into her parents' arms.

Kay was babbling on to Alex about something. Leah tried to tune back into the conversation. "I hope I get to meet your dad someday. He's absolutely my *favorite* dancer."

Alex favored Kay with a tolerant smile. "Oh, you will. He's due to guest with the Bay Area Ballet sometime this winter. I don't really keep track of his schedule." Alex leaned back against the doorframe and crossed her long arms over her thin chest. Very coolly she regarded Kay's pile of luggage. "I see you at least *intend* to stay here. You should show the judges all this stuff you brought. They won't have the heart to send you home." Between her accent and the tone of her voice, Leah couldn't tell if Alex was trying to be witty or somehow putting Kay down.

For a moment it seemed Kay couldn't tell either. She flashed Alex a puzzled look then began to laugh. She picked up a bag in each hand. "That's the idea!" she commented, starting down the hall. Leah started to follow her with another bag, but Kay called over her shoulder, "You go upstairs and get yourself settled. You've helped me enough, Leah. I can take it from here. Thanks."

Leah turned to Alex to introduce herself, but the words died on her lips. Alex wore a very smug expression as she watched Kay bounce down the hall toward her room. "She's a real original!" Alex commented. "A breath of fresh air. SFBA could use a girl like her."

Leah wasn't sure why, but the way Alex spoke made her blood boil. She sounded so superior and condescending. Leah clenched her teeth and gathered her own bags. Just because she was from somewhere more exotic than Pennsylvania, Alex didn't have the right to look down on a sweet person like Kay, or poke fun at her. Leah tilted her chin up in the air and with great dignity started up the next flight of steps.

"And who are you?" Alex's deep breathy voice rose up the stairs after her. Leah turned around and looked down at Alex. "Leah, Leah Stephenson," she replied. She clutched her bags tightly and ignored Alex's outstretched hand.

Alex arched one fine dark eyebrow. "Well, welcome to SFBA," she said with an offhanded shrug, then bent down and picked up Kay's last two bags. She started down the hall whistling the love theme from *Romeo and Juliet.*

As Leah made her way up the stairs, she wondered if all the students at the Academy were going to be as stuck-up and arrogant as Alex or as rude as James.

*   *   *

Leah stepped out into the cool foggy night. She inhaled the damp air. It felt fresh and soothing against her warm skin. "It's a beautiful night," she said to Pam. "I'm glad we decided to take a walk."

"Me too," Pam said. "I couldn't believe Kay actually wanted to hang around after dinner. That nerdy pianist friend of Sorokin's was too much. Do you think he's her boyfriend?" she asked in a low, gossipy voice. "A girl with looks like that could sure do better than him. I hope there are some boys worth looking at around here, more like that guy we ran into when we walked into the Academy. He was something else."

"You mean James?" Leah asked, not quite believing that any girl in her right mind would be attracted to such an obviously snobby and rude boy. But since she really didn't know him—or Pam—she gave a noncommittal reply. "I guess he's cute."

"Speaking of cute," Pam continued airily. "Kay is a walking definition of the word. She's such a *sweet* person. A little naive though."

Leah frowned as Pam rambled on. She liked Kay and didn't feel right talking about her behind her back.

Leah's lack of response didn't bother Pam. She just barreled on. "But then, Kay is so desperate to get tight with Alexandra because of her famous parents, she probably wouldn't notice if the house burned down around her. Not that I blame her. Alex's dad is pretty impressive, but still, she should smarten up. I mean, she just lost her cool so completely." Pam smoothed her thick hair over the top of her jacket and shook her head in dismay. "I've never seen anything like it. I went up to see her room before supper and she was barely unpacked but she had a framed publicity photo of Lynne Vreeland on her dresser already. What do you think of Vreeland?" Pam shot her question at Leah and studied her face intently.

Leah laughed uncomfortably. "Uh, Lynne Vreeland? I think she's great. Actually, she's one of my favorite dancers." She frowned, slightly put off by Pam's analysis of Kay, though there was a hint of truth to what she said. "And Kay just gets overly enthusiastic. I'm pretty impressed myself about the Sorokins," Leah admitted with a sigh. "I guess having famous dancer parents was an asset when Alexandra auditioned for this place."

"Auditioned?" Pam countered instantly. "Are you kidding? The school probably begged her to come. She doesn't have to be very good, you know. Companies will be banging her door down soon just to sigh her up. Russian defectors are such a big draw," she said knowingly.

Leah looked skeptical. "I don't know about that. She looks like a good dancer to me. And Russian training, especially at the Kirov school, is really incredible. Makarova and Nureyev came from there. You heard Alex over dinner. She told Kay she studied at the Vagonova Institute when she was six." Leah wanted to be fair. Just because she thought Alex was a snob didn't mean she might not be a really good dancer.

Talking about Kay and Alex with Pam didn't

feel right to Leah, so to change the subject she said, "Where are we going?" She felt as though she could walk all night. Although the boarding-house wasn't right on the bay, the air was sweet with a gentle sea breeze and she could hear the sound of foghorns bleating in the distance.

"Not far. I was quite serious about walking, you know, what I told Kay earlier today. It's bad for the knees."

Leah winced. Miss Greene had never told her anything like that and she wondered where Pam got her theories. She was used to long healthy hikes up into the hills with Chrissy and her knees had never bothered her one bit.

"My San Francisco guide book says this area's got lots of cool coffee houses, places with fabulously sinful chocolate desserts."

Leah could practically hear Pam lick her lips in the dark.

Pam took her arm and gave her a friendly shake. "Are you all game?" she asked in a conspiratorial whisper. "I almost never let myself do this, but I could go for something very chocolate and very fattening right now. Like a hot fudge sundae—yummy!" At the end of the block they came to a busy intersection. Pam looked around for a moment, then let out a little sigh of delight. "Can you believe that name, Cocoa-Nuts? That's where we just have to go."

They deposited themselves at one of the brown and white metal tables inside, and to Leah's relief Pam's pigout proved more modest than predicted. While Leah sipped her Perrier, Pam contented herself with a small scoop of chocolate ice cream and ogling everyone else's extravagantly gooey concoctions. "I really have to watch my figure," Pam complained. "I'm not like you. I can tell you can eat up a storm and never gain a pound. Every calorie I eat turns into fat, just like that!" She snapped her fingers.

Leah didn't contradict Pam. "I'm pretty lucky that way," she said, trying not to pay too much attention to a crowd of girls about their age giggling at a nearby table. They had the air of friends who had known one another a long time. Leah felt a funny tug at the back of her throat as she watched them. Suddenly her life at home seemed so long ago and far away. It was almost impossible to imagine she had left just that morning. She wondered vaguely what Chrissy was doing now. Probably hanging out with the crowd at Sneaky Pete's, eating too much ice cream and complaining about getting fat. It made Leah feel lonely to think of Chrissy, driving home the fact that Pam was still nearly a stranger. Of course, she probably could be a friend—so could Kay—if they all ended up in school together. But sitting in the middle of this noisy, crowded coffeehouse, Leah decided Chrissy was wrong. You didn't make friends just like that, in the wink of an eye. Leah stretched out her legs and dug her hands deep into the pockets of her pants. Thinking of home right now wasn't going to help a thing: not her audition, and not whatever final business had to be finished between her and Chrissy when she got back to San Lorenzo. She brushed a wisp of hair off her forehead and searched for something to say to get her mind off Chrissy and home. She swallowed hard and after a short pause continued lamely about diet. "I sort of burn stuff off. But I don't eat dessert very often."

"Now Kay, she's so tiny—" Pam shook her head sadly. "I bet she can't eat a thing. You know how it is."

Leah didn't know, but she certainly could imagine. Every ounce must show on the five-foot-one dancer. Kay probably had to keep her weight at just ninety pounds.

"Too bad she's so short." Pam shook her head ruefully and licked a drop of chocolate off the edge of her spoon.

"What's wrong with being short?" Leah asked. Talking to Pam left her feeling as if she didn't know the first thing about dancers and dancing.

"Oh, nothing. Except, well, there's not much demand for such cute little dancers. Not in most American companies. They take things like that into consideration, you know."

Leah wasn't sure she followed Pam's logic. "At the auditions, you mean," she asked.

"You got it!" Pam said knowingly. "She's got two strikes against her. And she hasn't even gone to class yet."

"I have a feeling she's a pretty good dancer, and being short won't hurt her one bit." Leah felt a sudden strong need to defend Kay.

"Oh, I don't doubt she can *dance*," Pam said quickly. "But dancing isn't what this is all about, is it?"

"Isn't it?"Leah was really confused now.

"Everyone here can dance. Didn't Diana say there were over one hundred applicants this year, just in the high school division? Kids come from all over the country, and believe me, schools send only their very best pupils."

"I guess that makes sense," Leah said with a sinking heart. For the third time that day she got the feeling the deck was already stacked against her. She wondered what Pam thought about her own chances of getting into the school. She was too afraid to ask. Pam seemed to know so much about how these auditions worked. Leah slumped slightly in her seat and had to wonder for a moment why she had bothered coming to San Francisco at all.

In the next few minutes Pam proceeded to analyze the other girls they had met over dinner at the boardinghouse. Sally Jenkins was too awkward to even be considered. Linda, on the other hand, looked promising. But that pale Katrina Gray looked positively anorexic.

That night Leah lay on top of her bed with the light on, unable to sleep. She curled her toes under the hem of her long cotton nightgown and held her pillow to her chest, wishing her cat, Misha, were there curled up beside her. Even with the window open the top floor room was cozy and comfortable. From the bed Leah could see the sweep of a harbor light circling the bay and the air smelled of the ocean and distant places. But tonight Leah longed for something familiar with the scent of home about it.

Her conversation with Pam had left her shaken. To think that just this morning she had actually believed, no matter what had gone wrong with Chrissy, no matter how guilty she felt about leaving her mom, she was going to get into SFBA and then all the tears and fears would be worth it. Now she wondered how anyone actually got into the school. What did the judges look for in a fifteen-year-old girl? Good training? A strong slim body? Charisma? Presence? Quality? Line? All the things that added up to talent? Leah didn't know. Pam said talent didn't count—not that much. But if talent didn't count, what did?

Leah rolled over onto her stomach and flicked out the light at last. She slipped between the crisp clean sheets, hugged her knees to her chest, and asked herself one more time. Was there anything about her that would make her one of Madame Preston's chosen few?

Chapter 7

The next morning Leah walked into the Academy's Red Studio and plopped herself down on the floor. Trying her best to look invisible, she began her warm-up stretches. She slowly curled her body forward over her outstretched legs and peered up at the roomful of dancers.

The other girls auditioning for the coveted fifteen places on the incoming high school program were easy to pick out: they all clustered at the back of the class, wearing pink tights and black leotards with narrow elastics tied around their waists and pink leather slippers—just like the dress code in the catalog had stated. The rest of the dancers were outfitted in a colorful hodge-podge of nylon warm-up pants, thick socks, sweaters, baggy shirts, weird suspenders. Leah figured they were members of the company or other professional dancers taking advantage of audition week's special Sunday class. Alexandra was there, too, and that boy, James. Leah wasn't surprised to see them talking together in the corner. She had a feeling they knew each other. Idly she wondered if James was Alexandra's partner. They certainly looked attractive together. Alexandra caught Leah's glance and smiled coolly in her direction. Leah didn't smile back. She looked away, wishing Pamela or Kay were there.

They had been assigned to Patrick's class in the Green Studio, and from the sound of music across the hall, Leah knew their class had already started. She was dying to see them dance, half out of curiosity to see if they were as good as she suspected, but also because she wanted them to be her friends. It would be terrible to have friends here whose dancing you didn't respect. But she'd have to wait until Madame Preston's audition class on Tuesday to check them out. Leah would catch up with them later in time for lunch. Pam had suggested a quick tour of Chinatown after class before heading back to the Academy for rehearsals later that afternoon.

Diana Chen walked into the room and Leah was relieved. At least she had met the teacher. Diana set a container of tea on the piano and clapped her hands together sharply. "Places please!"

Leah scrambled to her feet and hurried to claim a spot at the crowded barre. She sandwiched herself between two girls she'd already met at Mrs. Hanson's the night before: Linda Howe, a willowy black girl with enormous eyes and an elfin face, and Sally Jenkins, the girl from Iowa, who somehow looked all wrong in her dance clothes.

Leah glanced in the mirror and pulled down

the back of her leotard. Her hair was pinned up tidily. Her makeup was subtle but played up her fine features, and she wore her favorite turquoise studs that brought out the color of her eyes. She had dressed with particular care this morning. Miss Greene had warned her that no matter what anyone said, every move she made—particularly in class—would count toward her final score at the audition. As she caught Diana looking in her direction, she suddenly knew what Miss Greene had said was true.

She stood quietly at the barre, her heart pounding as she waited for Diana to demonstrate the opening combination of pliés. Diana scanned the room and smiled.

"Okay, you new girls, stop hiding in the back of the class. As I told you during orientation, you're not going to be judged until Tuesday. It would do you some good today to take advantage of the professional and more experienced dancers around you. Please arrange yourselves at the barre so you're not all clumped together. After all, dancers aren't supposed to be shy. Believe it or not, this is show biz!" Her bell-like voice was tinged with sarcasm.

Leah blushed, and joined the scramble to change places. To her dismay she ended up toward the front of the room across from Alexandra and behind James. A moment later the piano started and strains of Chopin filled the room.

Leah took a deep breath, assumed second position, and let her knees bend into a soft demi plié. At first her eyes were riveted on James's muscular back. She had never taken class with a boy before. His movements were broad and his timing slightly different from hers, but she was surprised at how well he moved. She wondered if he was already a professional dancer. She was surprised that such a rude, sharp person moved with such intense grace.

"Down-and-two-and-three-and-four and up-and—" Diana cruised the room, tapping one girl's bottom, poking a young man between his shoulder blades. Leah tensed as Diana approached, but she passed by without seeming to notice her. The pace of the music was slower than Leah was used to, forcing her to control her muscles until they were shaking at the end of her grand pliés in fifth.

For the next fifteen minutes Leah went through the barre exercises alternately challenged by the pace, then confused. In spite of her own struggle to keep up, she couldn't help but watch Alexandra across the way. Pam had been wrong. Alexandra was very good. She worked easily, with great concentration and flawless technique. Every tendu closed in a tight perfect fifth. Her back bends were soft and beautiful and deep. Her port de bras was broad and expansive. Watching her, Leah wished she were trying out for the Kirov school in Leningrad and not SFBA. She'd give anything to develop upper body movement like that. With or without famous parents, Alex was destined for a brilliant career. Leah was sure of it.

"Leah Stephenson. Pull that weight up off your hips!" Diana's sharp reprimand startled Leah. She bit her lip but continued the series of developpés.

"Sorry," she murmured, and blushed furiously as she tried to lift her weight off her supporting leg. It had never dawned on Leah that auditioning students would be corrected in class. From what she had read, new students weren't corrected that much at first, not until the teacher watched them work for several classes. Then she realized Diana hadn't said one word to any of the other new girls. Leah's heart stopped. Why had she picked on her? She must be the worst dancer there.

She fought back the impulse to run from the room. Giving up, just like that, would be letting Miss Greene down. Leah moistened her lips and blocked every thought from her head except the slow unfolding of her leg to the front, to the side, and to the back.

"Other side, please," Diana ordered. The music continued and Leah turned around at the barre. Somehow she got mixed up. She drew up her leg into a retiré and unfolded to the side first. She gritted her teeth and lowered her leg and started again.

The music stopped.

"Stephenson!" Diana called. Before Leah had a chance to turn around, she sensed the teacher coming up behind her. Diana was just her height and her eyes met Leah's with a challenge. "We're simply doing the same thing to the other side. It's not that hard. Watch Alexandra," Diana instructed. She tapped her hand against the barre and the pianist began a slow Schubert melody. Alexandra flashed Leah a curiously sympathetic look, then performed the exercise perfectly.

Leah was humiliated. At Hannah Greene's school it was Leah who was always called on to demonstrate. Of all the students for Diana to pick to give a demonstration, it had to be Alexandra Sorokin. Leah's faint distaste for the Russian girl irrationally flamed up into absolute dislike. What was wrong with all those professionals in the room? Why couldn't Diana demonstrate herself?

"Now you do it!" Diana ordered. She stood right next to Leah, watching her with an eagle eye. Leah glared briefly at the teacher, then recalled where she was. She suddenly remembered Miss Greene again. Everything counts. Everything. Maybe this was some kind of test. Leah had no way of knowing. Her chances of getting into the school were probably nil now. But she did have her pride. She took a deep breath, and when the music began, she blocked out every thought, every feeling, and listened with her whole body. She felt herself grow tall on her supporting leg. Unconsciously she mimicked Alexandra's perfect adagio movement. Each time she brought her working leg in she forced herself to pull up a little higher on her hip. At the end of the exercise she knew she had never done a better set of developpés in her life.

Diana didn't say a thing. She just walked away and asked the pianist to begin the music again so the whole class could go through the movement one more time.

The dressing room was crowded. Leah sat on a bench, dazed, too tired and dispirited to even change her clothes. Kay and Pam would just have to wait. If they went to Chinatown without her, Leah wouldn't even care. She wasn't exactly in the mood to compare notes about the morning class.

Linda walked up. Leah could see by the expression in her eyes she was about to console her. Leah braced herself. She wasn't in the mood for pity right then. "Don't be so hard on yourself," Linda said sweetly. "I think she was being a bit unfair."

Leah shrugged. Linda and the other girls meant well when they clustered around her after class and told her not to be discouraged. Linda meant well now. But how could she understand what Leah was feeling? Two times Diana had singled her out. The second time she had downright humiliated her by making her watch Alexandra. Leah's cheeks burned at the memory.

"She wasn't being unfair," Alex spoke up suddenly. She was over in a corner peeling off her leotard. She reached for a container of baby powder and dusted it on before yanking her sweater over her head. Today she was dressed all in white. She grabbed her stretch pants and sauntered toward Leah. Leah was uncomfortably aware the other girls were listening intently to what the Russian girl was saying. "She wasn't picking on you. She was giving you a compliment."

Leah rolled her eyes toward the ceiling. "Come off it!" She balled up her towel and tossed it in her bag. She stood up and faced Alexandra. "I'd say you're the one who got the compliment."

Alexandra arched one eyebrow and shrugged. "Not really. I'm a strong adagio dancer and I'm still a student. She wasn't about to ask one of the members of the company to demonstrate for you. But you know, it takes some people months to get noticed around here."

"That's not the kind of notice I feel like getting," Leah retorted.

"Correction in class is the best kind of notice a dancer can get," Alex said simply. The other girls had drifted away. The room was half empty now. Alex sat down on the bench and watched Leah as she pulled her overalls over her tights and leotard. "So what are you doing now?" she asked.

Leah spun around, startled by the question. Had she imagined it or did Alex actually sound friendly?

Before Leah could reply, Alex said, "I was thinking maybe you'd like to go out for lunch before your rehearsal. I could show you around the neighborhood."

Leah stepped back in surprise. "Lunch?" she repeated suspiciously, not sure how to react to Alex's invitation. Going out with Alex wasn't something she was sure she wanted to do, even if she could. She stared directly into the Russian girl's dark eyes, and decided this was a person to be careful of. Leah drew in her breath sharply and let out a tense laugh. "I guess I can't," she said.

The open, friendly expression immediately faded from Alex's face. "Oh," she said tersely.

Leah started to say she had other plans, but Alex grabbed her bag and swept out of the room before she could get out a word.

"Now, what was that all about?" Leah cried aloud, feeling vaguely guilty, as if she had just done something wrong. With a disgusted shake of her head she gathered her things and set off to find Kay and Pam. Alexandra Sorokin was the most peculiar person Leah had ever met, one minute remote and cold, friendly the next. Even though Alex was the one who had just walked off in a huff, Leah found herself feeling as if she were the one who had behaved badly. She stopped at the mirror just outside the dressing room and angrily tugged her brush through her long blond hair. With sharp gestures, she bunched it up into a ponytail.

Suddenly she felt all mixed up. How could you tell who was friendly around here and who wasn't? Pam seemed friendly, but she talked a lot behind the other girls' backs. She had probably told Kay her opinion of Leah's prospects as a dancer, something Kay was too polite to repeat to Leah's face. And Kay was warm enough, but what would she be like when the going got really tough? And Alexandra, even though she wasn't competition in the approaching audition, she promised to be competition if Leah ended up attending the school.

Halfway down the hall toward the stairs, Leah heard Alex's throaty laugh. She peered into the Blue Studio. There was Alex perched on the piano watching James practice pirouettes in front of the mirror. Leah hadn't heard the first part of Alex's conversation, but now her words rang out loud and clear into the hall. "—a sweetheart, but that Stephenson is so uptight. I can't wait until she faces Preston in class."

"Don't you wish you could be there!" James said, coming out of his pirouette and striking a haughty pose in front of the mirror. He admired himself a moment, then threw back his handsome head and let out a loud laugh.

"Look at these shoes. Aren't these just the coolest thing you all have *ever* seen!" Pamela cooed. Before Leah could protest, Pamela marched into the tiny boutique sandwiched between an acupuncturist and a steamy-windowed Chinese takeout shop.

Kay let out a tired sigh and leaned against the wall, working her ankle around in a circle. "Patrick's class this morning was a killer. There was an oversupply of boys in it, so we did lots of jumps. Pam loved it. She's got an incredible jump. She kept up with the guys and didn't even look tired. I bet *her* feet don't hurt." Kay's tired face brightened, and she poked Leah with her elbow. "You know, I've never had a class with guys in it before. Have you?"

"No," Leah said, "And I've never danced with a partner either."

"Pam has. She's been going to ballet camp in Massachusetts since she was ten. She told me all about it this morning. She's had pas de deux class for a couple of years now." Kay peeked around Leah's shoulder and tried to catch a glimpse of

Pam. "Pam can afford to spend all this time here. Her rehearsal's not scheduled until four. Mine's at three. How about you?" Kay sounded anxious.

"Same as you," Leah replied. "I want to get back and warm up. I've had enough of Chinatown." The whirlwind tour of the famous San Francisco district had been fun, but Leah's head was spinning from seeing so many new things. She wasn't as tired as Kay, at least not physically, but mentally she was drained. This was just the first day of audition week, and Leah wasn't sure how she'd make it through to the end, to dancing her variation in front of the judges. In the meantime, she had to act as if she were going to make it. She had to eat, drink, and sleep her steps. She was in no mood to be late for her first rehearsal with the pianist who'd accompany her. She pushed up her sleeve and checked the plastic Betty Boop watch Chrissy had given her for her last birthday. Two-fifteen. She flashed Pam an annoyed look through the glass door of the store.

Pam was leaning over the cluttered countertop chatting easily with the proprietor. He was counting change into her hand. Pam stopped him and pointed to another pair of strapped black cotton flats. Leah let out an exasperated sigh. "You'd think she was trying to make us late on purpose."

Just as Leah was about to go into the store to tell Pam she and Kay were leaving, Pam flounced out. "You won't believe these prices. I don't know what's the matter with you two. You're just crazy to pass up such bargains—"

"Pamela!" Leah cried impatiently. "Do you know what time it is?"

Pam shook her head. She gave an embarrassed shrug and pointed to her wrist. "Why, look. I forgot my watch today."

"Oh, never mind," Leah groaned. "Listen, we've got to get out of here. Kay and I are scheduled for rehearsals in forty-five minutes. Now, where are we exactly?" Leah looked around trying to figure out what direction they had come from after getting off the bus from school. With any luck they'd make it back just in time.

"My, you really are nervous. Don't you worry about a thing. I have a sixth sense when it comes to direction." Pamela guided Kay and Leah to the corner and made a right-hand turn onto a busy intersection. "Hey! I think we can even take one of these adorable cable cars!"

"I don't remember passing any cable cars on the way down here." Kay fumbled in her bag for change, and eyed the approaching vehicle suspiciously. "Don't you think we should ask where it's going?"

"Nonsense. I studied a map and guide book last night before I went to sleep. I know exactly where we are."

Leah was too tired to argue with Pam. She climbed up behind the other girls and clung to an overhead strap as the car careened down a steep hill. "This wasn't such a good idea after that big lunch," she complained, patting her stomach with her free hand. When she was a kid she had loved riding the cable cars, but at the moment the ride was making her seasick.

"Pamela." Kay's voice was shrill. "This is absolutely the wrong direction. Maybe you've got the time to waste, but I don't. Neither does Leah."

"Why, what do you mean?" Pamela sounded insulted. "Why I— Oh, no!" She put a hand to her mouth and groaned as the car approached the financial district. "You're right. We shouldn't be anywhere near these office buildings. We'd better get off at the next stop."

The three girls silently watched the cable car pull off. Kay turned to Pam accusingly. "Now what?" Her voice trembled and she rubbed her sleeve across her eyes. She was obviously on the brink of tears.

"Would you all just calm down." Pam stepped out onto the street. She waved down a cab. "This is my treat. I don't want you blaming poor little me if you're a tad late for your rehearsal."

Chapter 8

Leah peeled off her jeans and yanked on her leg warmers in record time. She was glad she hadn't bothered to take off her tights and leotard after that morning's class. Tying the pink satin ribbons on her shoes seemed to take an eternity. "Calm down," she told herself aloud in the empty third-floor changing room. "Just calm down. You're not that late." As rushed as she was, she vowed to warm up before practicing her variation. The accompanist would just have to wait another couple of minutes. Cursing Pam and her stupid shopping spree one last time, she sped down the hall to her assigned practice room.

Just before she got to the door, she stopped and forced herself to at least *look* calm. She wished that everything she had had to do since coming to the Academy didn't feel so new to her. She had no idea what a person did in a private session with an accompanist, but since it was her variation they were about to practice, she figured she should at least give the impression she was in charge. She gulped down a deep breath of air, drew herself up very tall, and opened the glass-windowed door. She wondered if the correct thing to do was ask the pianist's name.

An upright piano loomed large against the far wall. The accompanist was hidden behind the open pages of the *San Francisco Examiner*. Leah paused in the doorway and cleared her throat. The paper rattled and a young brown-haired man with glasses peered around the edge. He reached for a container of coffee and took a sip, then folded the newspaper in a precise, neat fashion.

"You're here," he said flatly, looking up at the wall clock. "I can't give you extra time, someone else is due at the stroke of four." When he didn't bother to introduce himself, Leah decided not to ask his name.

Her stomach knotted up. She had half expected he couldn't extend her session. Because of Pam's mistake she was going to miss out on precious practice time. A momentary wave of dislike for Pam swept over her, but then she realized being late was partly her fault for not speaking up when she was pretty certain the cable car wouldn't take them in the right direction. The redhead was so cocky and sure of herself, she hadn't even thought about the consequences of getting lost. Well, there was nothing to do about it now. Leah marched over to the barre and said, "I understand about your schedule, but I have to warm up first." She sounded so calm, she could hardly believe the words came out of her own mouth.

The accompanist didn't reply. He shrugged and unfolded his paper again. "Whenever you're ready."

Leah fought to keep her mind on her warm-up routine. Dancing on cold muscles was just begging for trouble. All she needed now was an injury before she even got a chance to take Madame Preston's class. She finished up a brief round of tendus and concentrated on her battements. Within a few minutes her muscles felt stretched again. She hadn't really warmed up enough, but with any luck she wouldn't get hurt.

She pulled her music from her dance bag and set it on the piano. The accompanist closed his paper and opened the score. His high pale forehead wrinkled as he read her name. "Oh, it's you," he commented, then pushed the clear plastic frames of his eyeglasses up on his nose and peered at her with small close-set eyes that seemed to be colorless. She stepped back self-consciously.

"We haven't met before," she stated, then realized he did look vaguely familiar.

"Uh, no, we haven't. But I heard about you after Diana's class today," he said with a noncommittal shrug. "My name's Robert." He placed his thin bony hands on the keyboard and looked back up at Leah. "Well, are you ready?"

Leah nodded and walked over to a corner of the narrow studio, still unable to place him. She was pretty sure she didn't know him, and it unnerved her to hear that people had been talking about her poor performance during the morning class. She struck her opening pose and waited for the music to start.

But when Robert began to play, she didn't move. The music stopped. She stayed rooted to the spot. Suddenly she knew exactly who Robert was—Alexandra's friend, the nerdy guy Pam had noticed hanging out in Mrs. Hanson's living room the night before. The color rushed to Leah's cheeks. Alexandra must have been the one who had told him how she'd messed up in Diana's class. She had absolutely no right to gossip about Leah like that. The more she found out about Alex, the less she liked her. Leah pursed her lips and said in a clear tight voice, "Please begin again."

This time she didn't miss her cue. The delicate strains of her variation from *Sleeping Beauty* brought her reluctant feet to life. At first she felt like a wind-up doll. She had done the steps so many times that although her cheeks were burning and her mind was racing—filled with imagined comebacks she would hurl at the Russian girl the minute she got her alone—Leah got halfway through the piece without making a mistake.

Then she caught a glimpse of herself in the wall mirror. She looked stiff and tight. All her anger had settled into her neck and shoulders. The angle of her head was all wrong and her hands looked like Ping-Pong paddles. Miss Greene's corrections echoed in her brain: the music held all the hints to how the steps should be danced. Robert might be one of Alexandra's friends, but at least he played the piano beautifully, phrasing the variation just as Leah's body yearned to dance it. Robert's rendition was far better than the practice tape Miss Greene had made for her from the music collection at the San Lorenzo Public Library. With a great effort of will Leah forced herself to focus her mind on nothing but the music. All at once her dancing changed. Her little hops on pointe softened, her arms loosened, and she felt her whole body grow light and airy. She forgot about Alexandra, the audition, Madame Preston, Pam's irresponsible antics. At that moment nothing existed but the music and the dance. Within seconds she reached the ending pose. She sustained the final arabesque easily without a wobble. She felt as if she could stand on one toe for hours.

Just as she dropped off pointe, she heard the sound of voices at the door. Leah spun around and looked over her shoulder in time to glimpse the back of Pam's head as she headed away from the rehearsal studio. Then her eyes met Alexandra's. Alexandra stared at her a moment, then silently applauded, her slender, nigh-cheekboned face widening into an inscrutable smile. Alex turned to the boy standing next to her, and Leah's hands clenched into a fist. It was James. When he saw Leah staring at him, he arched one thick dark eyebrow high and had the nerve to wink.

Leah fumed inwardly and turned away from them. She marched over to the barre and yanked a towel out of her bag. She made a fuss of wiping off her face, although she had barely worked up a sweat yet. "Can we do that again?" she asked in a loud voice. She was still bent over, trying to gather her wits about her. Her audition program was supposed to be a secret; her practice session was supposed to be private. The mistakes she made in this room weren't for public consumption—or comment.

As she took her opening pose, her cheeks were still flaming. She willed herself not to look back toward the door. The music started and Leah began to dance again, this time concentrating on perfecting the intricate port de bras that gave the variation its special charm. As she stepped into one of the slow attitude turns, she glanced toward the door. No one was there. Alexandra and James were gone.

Leah was able to relax now that she knew she wasn't being watched, but she was still furious. Tonight she'd tell Alex off, even if she had to confront her over dinner. Having a friend like Pam sneak a peek at her variation was one thing, but Alex had no right to spy on her.

"*All* the tapes of *Sleeping Beauty* are out?" Leah stood at the information desk in the Academy's basement library not quite sure she'd heard right. Before she left rehearsal Robert had told her about the extensive videotape collection in the school library. He had specifically said there were at least three versions of *Sleeping Beauty*, including one of Margot Fonteyn. Leah's variation was on that tape and Robert had suggested she might find it helpful to study it.

"Sorry, dear." The dancer covering the desk double-checked a list scribbled on a yellow sheet of paper. "Every tape is out. I don't know who took what though. I just got here a little while ago." Leah didn't move. She wasn't quite sure what to do next. The librarian gave her a sympathetic look. "Things get crazy around here during audition week," he continued. "One hundred of you girls, every one of you dying to look at these tapes. *Sleeping Beauty* in particular is quite handy in the variation department. I bet everybody and her mother dances something from that."

Leah returned his smile weakly. She had never imagined anyone else would come to the audition and dance what she had come to feel was "her" variation. Leah could see now clear as day that her variation was the perfect length for an audition. It was also a simple one, technically. The difficulty lay in interpretation, and interpretation was Leah's strong point. But Leah had no doubt that half the Academy hopefuls in this room were as good at it as she was. She shuddered at the prospect of being compared to any one of the other students dancing the very same variation.

"If you want to look at some books while you're here, I'll let you know when the tapes are returned."

Leah thanked him, but didn't feel very encouraged as she strolled over to the stacks. She could kick herself for having stopped for tea after her rehearsal. It was after five now and Mrs. Hanson had told the girls to be home promptly for dinner at six-fifteen. That gave her less than an hour before she had to get back to the boardinghouse. Even if the tape did turn up, she wouldn't have time to watch it. Leah rounded the first shelf of stacks, trailing her finger along the spines of famous dancer biographies.

"What are you doing here?" a familiar voice gasped.

Leah found herself eye-to-eye with a red-faced Pamela Hunter.

Pam quickly hid something behind her back, then dropped her bag. Pencils, books, cassette tapes, makeup, toe shoes, a white towel, a hairbrush—everything spilled out onto the gray linoleum floor.

"Pam, what's wrong?" Leah asked with concern, noticing how flustered and upset Pamela looked. Leah bent down to help her gather her things, and didn't see Pamela tuck a videotape behind some books on a nearby shelf.

"Wrong?" Pam said shrilly. She ran her fingers through her long red hair and took a deep breath. With a forced smile she looked directly into Leah's eyes, and said more calmly, "Why, nothing's wrong. Whatever in the world gave you that idea?"

Leah shrugged and Pam went on in a more controlled, almost silly voice. "So what exactly *are* you doing here?"

Leah wrinkled her nose and slumped back against the shelf. She let out a sigh and explained her fruitless attempt to study a tape of her variation. "Would you believe it? *Every single version* of that ballet is being looked at at this moment." Leah threw her hands up in the air and gave a little despairing laugh. "The worst part is that by the time Madame Preston gets to watch me dance that variation, she'll probably be sick of it, unless I luck out and get the first draw on the audition schedule."

Pam shifted uncomfortably and rummaged in her bag for her brush. Holding an elastic band between her teeth, she pulled her hair back and began braiding it, her fingers flicking like little whips. "Why, Leah," she mumbled through her closed mouth, "*Sleeping Beauty*'s got about a million variations. I doubt that anyone will be doing the exact same one as you."

Leah straightened up and clapped her hand to her forehead. "That's what the librarian said." She started to laugh. "I think the prospect of all this competition is beginning to get to me," she admitted. "All I could picture was being one of a chorus line of ballerinas doing the exact same steps. It's kind of hard to imagine I'd get picked over someone else if that were the case."

"I'll bet it is," Pam muttered under her breath.

Leah didn't quite catch her words. "What did you say?"

"Huh? Oh, nothing."

"So what are you doing here?" Leah asked.

Pam looked around anxiously. She dropped her voice to a soft whisper and said, "You won't tell, will you?"

Leah shook her head, wondering what in the world Pam was being so mysterious about.

Pamela paused before revealing her secret. "I'm killing time," she murmured so softly Leah could barely hear her.

"What?" Leah said in a normal voice.

"Shhh!" Pam put a warning finger to her lips. She rolled her green eyes up toward the ceiling and motioned Leah closer. Leah bent her head next to Pam's.

"This accompanist I got, well, he's kind of cute, and he—"

Leah's innocent eyes widened. "He asked you out?" she whispered hoarsely. From something Diana had said during orientation, Leah vaguely suspected dating an Academy employee was against the rules.

"Yes, yes, that's it. And he offered to spend a little extra practice time with me first. So I have to wait until the school clears out and I'll get to work a bit longer with him in a studio."

"But, Pam," Leah said, sounding worried. "Mrs. Hanson was pretty clear about wanting us back at the boardinghouse by six-fifteen. She said it was some kind of audition week regulation."

"Oh, Leah, he's sooo cute," Pam drawled. She leaned back against the shelf and emitted a dramatic sigh. "So can you do me a favor and not tell anyone where I am."

"You want me to lie?" Leah looked horrified.

"No, of course not." Pam looked offended. "Just don't say you saw me here. Okay?"

Leah hesitated.

"I'd only ask a friend to do me a favor like this," Pam begged.

"Okay, so I won't say I saw you, but you're going to get in trouble."

"Oh, don't worry about me," Pam said breezily. "I can take care of myself."

Chapter 9

For the third time in the past five minutes Mrs. Hanson put down her fork and looked up at the grandfather clock. "I can't imagine where Pamela is!" she said in a worried voice, then glanced around the dining room table. Leah felt the boardinghouse proprietor's eyes rest on her, and the color rushed to her cheeks. It was nearly seven, and the girls had returned to the boarding-house after their first full day of class and re-hearsals too exhausted to talk much. Tonight's atmosphere, unlike yesterday's, was fairly subdued.

Leah avoided Mrs. Hanson's eyes and suddenly resented Pam for not letting her speak up. Mrs. Hanson was really worried, and Leah felt it was all her fault. Knowing Pam was on a date, even if she shouldn't be, would put Mrs. Hanson's mind at rest. But Leah had promised not to tell. She looked down at her plate and jabbed her fork hard into a carrot.

She just hoped Mrs. Hanson wouldn't ask her outright if she knew where Pam was. She was a terrible liar and always had been, ever since she was a kid and got caught stealing apricots from Mr. Calabrese's orchard. She had lied then about helping down a cat that was stuck up a tree, but no one had believed her. Of course it hadn't helped any that no cat was in sight and her pockets were stuffed with ripe fruit.

"Didn't you and Kay have lunch with Pam today?" Sally asked, looking up from her plate.

All eyes turned in Leah's direction. "Uh, yes. We did. But that was at lunchtime," she said, knowing that sounded very dumb. She caught Alexandra's eye and remembered Pam had been with Alex and James and had watched her rehearse with them. "She was all right this afternoon. I saw her head off to rehearsal about four or so. I'm sure she's fine, Mrs. Hanson," Leah said, glaring meaningfully at Alexandra. Alex could have said something too. Leah had planned to confront Alex over dinner about watching her practice session and gossiping about her behind her back. But now she was just too tired. Trying to argue when she could barely sit up straight seemed like a pretty poor idea.

Alex returned Leah's glare with a puzzled frown, then shrugged and helped herself to more salad.

Leah looked away. Kay and Katrina Gray were holding a private conversation at the end of the table. From the few words that drifted down toward Leah, she gathered Katrina was talking about her home in northern Vermont. The frail-looking girl interested Leah. She was just the sort Leah imagined being ordered to ballet lessons at the age of eight by a family doctor because she had

asthma and needed the slow, healthful strength-
ening ballet afforded. Lots of talented dancers
started that way. Watching her, Leah's face filled
with concern. Maybe Pam's diagnosis last night
after dinner was right. Instead of eating, Katrina
was pushing her peas from one side of her plate
to the other, and it looked as though she hadn't
touched a thing. Maybe she looked so frail because she *was* anorexic. The thought had barely
formed in Leah's mind, when Katrina's warm, pleasant laugh filtered down to her end of the table.

Suddenly Leah decided Pam's dire predictions
weren't true. The Vermont girl wasn't anorexic.
She was just too exhausted and nervous to eat.
Leah felt that way, and probably everyone else at
the table did too. They all looked ready to drop.

The front door opened and closed quickly with
a bang. Mrs. Hanson jumped up and poked her
head out into the hall. "Pamela! Where have you
been?"

Leah held her breath. She glanced at the clock
and frowned. Pamela had just been on the short-
est date in history.

Pamela appeared in the entrance to the dining
room. She caught Leah's eye and raised her eyebrows in an unspoken question. Leah gave a discreet shake of her head. Pam's shoulders relaxed
in relief. Leah was glad she hadn't given Pam
away and couldn't wait to hear exactly what had
happened with the accompanist.

"Pam?" Mrs. Hanson stood in the doorway, tapping her foot, waiting for an explanation.

Pam's haughty face melted into an apologetic

expression. "You all were worried about *me*?" she drawled. "Well, I was, uh, at school." Mrs. Hanson's frown deepened. Pam hurried on. "After rehearsal I just didn't feel all that well and I lay down in the dressing room." She paused and her eyes darted quickly around the table. No one seemed about to contradict her so she continued. "And I guess I just fell asleep. I only woke up now," she said in an innocent, apologetic voice.

What an actress! Leah thought. She lowered her eyes to her plate and tried to keep the smile off her lips. She felt bad that Mrs. Hanson was swallowing Pam's crazy story, but she couldn't help but be impressed at Pam's ease in manufacturing it.

Pam was still rambling on, managing to sound perfectly pathetic. "And Mrs. Hanson"—she turned her large green eyes on the landlady—"I'm so sorry you all worried that I'm late. I just feel so bad. I have this terrible headache." She rubbed her forehead gingerly and leaned back against the doorframe. "I hope you don't mind, after you went to all this trouble preparing dinner, but I can't possibly eat a single bite. I'd just like to take some tea to my room."

"Poor thing," Mrs. Hanson's worried face softened. "Audition week is tough on you young girls. Too much pressure," she mumbled, shaking her head in annoyance. "That's one reason we want you back here after your first day's workout. Go right to your room, dearie. I'll bring you some tea in a minute. A hot bath might help too," she suggested on her way to the kitchen.

"Headache, ha!" Alex exclaimed. "That girl is too much." She cast a scathing glance in the direction of Pam's room and said, "When *I* have a headache, I can't spend all that time in the library watching videotapes."

"Maybe that's what gave her the headache," Katrina said, pouring herself a glass of milk.

"Maybe. But I wouldn't make a wager on it," Alex said in her slightly awkward English.

Kay giggled. "I wouldn't *bet* on it!" she corrected her. Alex thanked Kay with a sheepish smile.

Leah sat back in her chair and twirled her napkin between her hands. She checked to see that Mrs. Hanson was out of earshot, then studied Alexandra a moment in silence. Finally she asked her in a very controlled voice, "And why, might I ask, were you *spying* on poor Pam in the library?"

"Spying?" Alexandra repeated with an innocent look that turned Leah's stomach.

"You know what I mean," Leah said curtly. "Watching her every move, checking her out."

"Did anyone ever tell you you're paranoid?" Alex grumbled. She poked at a piece of spinach on her plate and regarded Leah thoughtfully. "I was in the library too. Half the school was in the library this afternoon. Weren't you?"

Leah turned crimson. Alex had known all along Pam was in the library. And she knew Leah knew, but like Leah, Alex hadn't told Mrs. Hanson when she asked where Pam was.

"I didn't see Pam." Kay spoke up from her end of the table.

"Oh, she was there. When I went to see if there was a video of your dance, Pam was in one of the booths, hogging a whole stack of tapes."

"Tapes?" Leah frowned, the information suddenly registering. Pam hadn't said anything about watching tapes. She said she had just been killing time until she could meet the pianist who had asked her out.

"Aren't the tapes great," Kay commented enthusiastically. "Alex finally located one of my variation and it really helped me. I forgot half my steps during my practice session, but once I saw it danced again, they all came back to me." Kay looked toward the older girl with admiring eyes.

Alex laughed. "Oh, you would have figured it out yourself sooner or later. Audition nerves make people forget which is their right foot and which their left."

Leah didn't know what surprised her more: Alex's story about Pam looking at tapes, when it was perfectly obvious Pam hadn't been doing any such thing, or the fact that snotty Alex had been helping Kay. She could tell from the way Kay and Alex were talking that they had somehow become very friendly in the past couple of hours. Leah suddenly felt left out and a little confused. Had Alexandra Sorokin come down from her pedestal to help another girl? That didn't quite fit the picture Leah was getting of Alex as a competitive, self-centered know-it-all. She looked over at Alex, distrust written all over her face.

"But why in the world would Pam lie about being in the library and watching tapes after her rehearsal?" Sally wondered aloud.

Alex leaned back in her chair and thoughtfully peeled an orange she plucked out of the fruit bowl. "Yes, why in the world?" she murmured, glancing at Leah.

Leah met Alex's gaze and didn't flinch. Alex must have suspected Leah had a pretty good idea where Pam had gone after the library. She had probably seen them talking. But Leah would be darned if Alex would get her to betray Pam's trust. "Beats me!" she said with a casual shrug of her shoulders.

With that Leah pushed back her chair and stretched her arms over her head. "I don't know about the rest of you, but I think Pamela has the right idea. I'm going upstairs to take a long bath, then crawl right into bed. Tomorrow's the last day before class with Madame Preston, and I for one have a lot of work to do."

She tossed her long blond hair off her shoulders and marched out of the dining room, avoiding Alexandra's gaze.

Upstairs she pulled off her clothes and settled into a tubful of bubble bath. The other girls hadn't left the dining room yet, so she figured she could indulge in a long hot soak without being accused of hogging the bathroom. Layer by layer, she felt the day's anger, tension, and exhaustion float away in the warm, fragrant water. She lay back against the cool porcelain of the antique claw-footed tub and began counting the fish that swam in schools across the blue and green wallpaper.

Counting fish, or flowers, or bunches of grapes on the wallpaper was an old trick she had discovered back home when she was nine years old, just after her father died. Back then it would stop her from hurting, at least temporarily. She'd get so mesmerized by the designs that she could let go of whatever problem was on her mind. She got into the habit of counting things whenever she was tired, depressed, or worked up over a step she couldn't learn. Friday night it had worked when she couldn't stop crying about leaving her mother. And it was working now.

Leah hooked her toe under the old-fashioned bathtub plug and popped it up. The water gurgled down the drain, washing away most of her cares. She got up and wrapped a thick fluffy towel around her slender body. She wiped the steam off the mirror and peered at her reflection. Her cheeks glowed a healthy pink from the bath. But the blue eyes that met her glance looked sad. Leah sighed and pressed her forehead against the glass. The clatter of feet on the stairs told her the other girls were heading toward their rooms. They'd be wanting the bathroom soon. But she stayed a bit longer, not moving, trying to dissect her feelings.

Her emotions ran strong and deep, but she was no good at putting them into words, even to herself. When she danced they all spilled out of her in a torrent: her anger, her joy, her fear, her pride, her love for everything and everyone around her. Right now she had a tight, scary sensation in the middle of her chest that her long bath and fish-counting hadn't loosened at all. And she couldn't quite put her finger on what was really bothering her.

She pulled the elastic from her ponytail and shook her hair loose. She combed her fingers through the tangles and reached for her robe. Chrissy. Her mom. The audition. Diana's put-down in class. Goofing off in Chinatown. Being late for her session with Robert. Alexandra spying on her during rehearsal. Why, she had a million good reasons to feel this upset. But as she stepped into the hallway, there was only one thing on her mind: the sharp, precise picture Alex drew of Pamela at the library watching tapes, and Pamela never mentioning tapes at all. Leah snuggled into the thick folds of her purple terry-cloth robe and walked back to her room trying to solve the puzzle. It just didn't make sense.

Leah entered her room and threw herself down on the bed, then sat up suddenly and hugged her pillow to her chest. "What's the matter with me?" she whispered into the pillowcase. Alex's accusation at the dinner table suddenly rang true. Only two days at the Academy and she was getting to be as paranoid as all those dancers she'd read about in a recent exposé of life behind the gilded curtain. Just because tapes were in use at a library, and Pam had some silly secret romance going on behind Mrs. Hanson's back, Leah was feeling all uptight and scared and threatened. She flopped down on her pillow and stared up at the ceiling. After a moment she turned off the light but lay there wide-eyed, her thoughts spinning around in her head like a merry-go-round.

Her mind kept turning back to Pam: Pam in the library, looking so flustered and confused when they ran into each other in the stacks. Leah sat up with a start. How peculiar. Pam hadn't said a word about her dancing, about watching her variation through the window of the rehearsal room. Remembering this, Leah felt hurt and a little let down. Alex hadn't said anything either, but Alex wasn't a friend. Sharing Pam's secret had made Pam seem like a friend. And a friend would have said something, anything, unless, of course, Leah had danced so badly, even a friend wouldn't tell her the truth.

Leah rolled over on her side and started to cry. But after the first few tears she sat up and dangled her feet over the bed. She brusquely rubbed the tears off her cheeks, and raked her hands through her hair. Abruptly she stood up. She walked over to the window, and shivered slightly in the breeze that wafted through the curtain. What in the world was happening to her? What Pam thought about her dancing, what anyone outside of Madame Preston thought about her dancing, shouldn't matter one bit. Hadn't Miss Greene told her that? Hadn't she said not to pay attention to anyone else? Not to their dancing, not to their opinions. Miss Greene had thought Leah was good enough to get into SFBA, and Hannah Greene knew a little more about what made a good dancer than Alex or Pam or James. Leah just had to believe that.

Turning away from the window, Leah gathered the hem of her nightgown into her hand and under her breath hummed the music to her variation. Step by step she marked it out, her body recreating each nuance of her performance this afternoon. When she finished, she stood very still at the foot of her bed. No, she hadn't danced badly. And yet Pam hadn't said a word about seeing her. But Leah wasn't there to get compliments from Pam or anyone else. She was here to become a great dancer and her business was to perform her audition piece as best she could, to make it close to perfect. Tomorrow after class she'd go back to the library before anyone else had a chance to get there. It would inspire her to watch that tape of Fonteyn.

She felt very free and light once she'd made her decision. Nothing and no one around here was going to bother her anymore. Leah was determined to follow Miss Greene's advice.

But as she climbed back into bed she still was thinking about Alexandra and her story about Pam hogging the tapes. Pam hadn't been watching them. Alex must have made it all up. But why? As Leah closed her eyes and drifted off to sleep, she pictured the dark-eyed girl's dramatically beautiful face. Although she was critical, caustic, and snobby, Leah had a strong feeling Alexandra Sorokin never lied.

Chapter 10

None of the tapes had been rewound.
Monday morning after class, Leah sat in one of
the tiny video studios tucked in a corner of the
Academy library and tried to digest that fact. She
was the first person in the library today. The guy
at the desk had recognized her and handed her
the stack of tapes with a big smile. "Today you're
at the head of the class!" He grinned as she
quickly made her way to the viewing booth.

Leah fingered each of the cassettes in turn: the
Kirov and Royal Ballet versions of *Sleeping Beauty;*
the tape of Fonteyn's variations. Each tape was
stopped at exactly the point where Leah's audition variation ended. She shuddered and drew
her feet up beneath her on the chair. Her deter-
mination not to let anything bother her anymore
had vanished. She gnawed the inside of her lip
and wondered why it should upset her so much
that someone had been studying her variation.

An hour later, walking across the lawn to the
audition week orientation lunch, Leah was still
preoccupied with her problem. Between class and

now she had just had time to watch the tape of
Fonteyn twice. But despite her best efforts she
had barely seen a step the great ballerina danced.
All she could think about was how unfair it was
that she would have to compete so directly with
so many girls. She wished Miss Greene had let
her choose an unusual variation like the one Pam
was doing from *La Bayadère*. Or she could have
choreographed her own piece, like Linda and
Katrina had.

"Hey, Leah!" Linda called out as she jogged
across the grass to Leah's side. "You didn't change
your clothes," she exclaimed, pointing to Leah's
pink tights peeping beneath her cropped striped
pants. Linda was wearing shorts and a brightly
patterned blouse and carrying a sunhat in one
hand. She rubbed her arm with her other hand
and gave a dramatic shiver. "Come to think of it,
you might have had the right idea. I thought it
was always warm here."

Leah smiled and looked around the crowded
lawn. Every one of the hundred girls auditioning
seemed to be hovering around the picnic tables.
Diana, Patrick, the guy from the library, and other
members of the company and faculty were there,
too, trying to make the prospective students feel
at home. Madame Preston, however, was nowhere
in sight. As Patrick had mentioned in class this
morning, she kept herself cloistered from the new
students until auditions were over. She wanted
her first impression of the girls to be of their
dancing, not of how they talked or socialized.

"I don't know about you, but I'm starved!" Linda

gestured toward the table. Girls were walking away with plates heaped with salad, fruit, cheese, and bread. "I'm going to take advantage of this feast to pig out. Coming?" she asked, waiting for Leah to join her.

Leah shook her head. "I couldn't eat a thing." She had no appetite at all.

"Nerves!" Linda diagnosed, then waved and headed off. "See you later," she called back over her shoulder. Leah started to smile, but her mouth turned down in a frown when she noticed James coming toward her. He had on a bathing suit and a towel was draped casually over one muscular shoulder. Leah looked around for a convenient place to disappear. She braced herself as he approached.

"Hi!" he said, as friendly as could be.

Leah did a double-take. "Hi, yourself." She turned around and headed toward the center of the crowd.

James followed behind her. "I just wanted to tell you how much I liked your dancing the other day, the way you performed your variation. You really show promise." Although what he said was a compliment, the way he said it didn't sound very nice. Until Leah had met James, she hadn't understood what it meant to be talked down to.

She faced him, frantically searching her mind for a comeback. His dark hair was wet from the pool and he slicked it back with his hand. He looked at her very intently, and his eyes seemed to bore right through her. Leah felt very uncomfortable, like a specimen under a microscope. She clenched her fists. Who was this guy anyway? He couldn't be much older than her. She found out from one of the other girls he was just a student too. What right did he have to judge her, even if his critique was a positive one? Doesn't anybody look at anyone else around here without sizing them up? she thought defensively. Out loud she said. "Thank you, but you shouldn't have been watching. That was private practice time."

The cutting edge to her voice was completely lost on James. "Oh," he said, reaching over to a table for a container of juice. "Nothing's that private around here. The school's pretty small, you know. Everyone knows everything about everyone else."

Before Leah could reply to that, Pam walked up. She was wearing a snug green tank top and a pair of pink pedal pushers. She stepped right in front of Leah and introduced herself. "My name's Pamela Hunter," she cooed. "Aren't you Alexandra's friend, James?"

Leah's eyes bulged. What was Pam doing, throwing herself at a guy like that?

James barely took notice. He stepped to the side and quite deliberately focused his attention on Leah. "So, where are you from?" he asked, again looking right into Leah's eyes.

"Atlanta," Pam answered before Leah could even open her mouth. She rested her hand lightly on James's arm and batted her long dark lashes. "She's just a local," she said, looking over at Leah with a condescending smile.

Leah's mouth fell open. "Pamela!" That Pam was interested in James was obvious, and Leah couldn't have cared less. The arrogant dancer wasn't exactly her cup of tea, but Pam's aggressive behavior shocked her.

"Well, you all are from California, from one of those little towns where they grow lettuce or garlic or something like that."

"I'm from San Lorenzo, and they grow artichokes there," Leah replied, not knowing if she was annoyed because responding to Pam meant answering James's question or because Pam was acting so pushy.

James arched his eyebrows and gave Leah a knowing smile. "I'd say they grow pretty impressive dancers there too."

Pam's lovely face darkened. She glared at Leah, then instantly her expression changed. "I believe he thinks that's a compliment," she said in a confiding, sugary tone. "Comparing you to some dumb vegetable." She playfully tugged James's towel and grabbed Leah by the arm. "Let's get out of here. This is definitely not the kind of guy who knows how to talk to girls."

Leah was too shocked to protest as Pam dragged her away from James. She was just as happy to get away from the boy. He had said nothing but nice things to her, but he somehow had a way of making nice things sound nasty. On the other hand, Pam had just acted truly obnoxious and Leah's gut instinct was to get as far away from her as possible. But Pam wasn't going to let her. She held Leah's arm tightly and began talking about that morning's class. She went on and on about what a great teacher Diana was, how absolutely hopeless Kay was at doing simple chaîné turns, and how that tall girl from Kansas was as gawky as a duck, and had the nerve to try to dance a variation from *Swan Lake* for her audition piece Wednesday. Not once did Pam mention her secret date of the night before.

That night after dinner everyone gravitated to Kay's room. Or almost everyone. Pamela had called Mrs. Hanson to say she'd be rehearsing late in one of the school studios and Alexandra had gone to the movies with James and Robert and a couple of other Academy students, taking advantage of one of the last few nights of their vacation.

Next week school reopened for the fall term and most of the regular students would be back. Leah looked around the room wondering if she, Kay, Linda, Sally, or Katrina would still be around then.

Kay sat with her leg propped up on the desk next to her framed photo of Lynne Vreeland. She arranged the ice pack on her ankle and settled back to mend a pair of tights. She had twisted her ankle slightly coming off a pirouette in class today. The injury wasn't serious, but Kay's usually merry face looked worried. Tomorrow was the audition class with Madame Preston. There'd be several audition classes running through the day. Kay, Leah, Pam, and Katrina were scheduled for ten A.M. That didn't give Kay's foot much time to mend. Kay had been telling everyone about Alexandra: how she'd spent all afternoon coaching her through her variation. Leah listened carefully. Had she been wrong about Alexandra? Every time she talked to the Russian girl she got the impression she was an incurable snob, keeping her distance from the other girls, silently criticizing them. But Kay's Alexandra didn't seem like that at all.

And Pam, who had seemed like a friend at first, was beginning to give her the creeps. The way she had acted with James was pretty disgusting. Leah had tried to dismiss that incident as the normal behavior of someone who was boy crazy, but some instinct told her there was more to it than that. The way she had almost physically pushed Leah aside was astonishing. Leah was beginning to get the distinct impression that Pam was the kind of girl determined to let nothing stand in her way. Once she set her mind to something, she got it, and how she got it just didn't matter.

And there was the way Pam would constantly put everyone down. It had bothered Leah that first night, when they went out for coffee, but Leah had decided that Pam merely had a passion for gossip. But now that Pam hadn't said one kind word about anybody yet, Leah was beginning to change her mind. Leah had gotten stuck with her all afternoon, and by the time she was finally able to escape the party, she had felt dishonest looking any other girl in the eye. According to Pam, not one girl there to audition was any good at all.

Leah did a couple of neck rolls to loosen the tension in her shoulders. She had a hunch there was more to Pam than met the eye, and the feeling was growing inside that the more she learned about the redheaded dancer, the less she was going to like her. The realization she might have misjudged Pam so badly really shook Leah's confidence. Nothing at SFBA was the way it seemed, just as nothing about it seemed to make any sense. Leah just hoped this atmosphere didn't prevail after auditions. She had to think that it was just from nerves and paranoia. Even she wasn't exempt from contributing to the uncomfortable air that surrounded them all. Hadn't she checked everyone out as if they were just a bunch of thoroughbreds lined up at the starting gate for a do-or-die race? Every girl's dream was on the line here. Leah seriously wondered if any of them could really ever be friends. A couple of days in this environment and anyone's head would begin to spin. Before Leah had come to SFBA she had thought she was good at understanding people, but here her judgment was blurred. No one was just a friend, and as of tomorrow, *everyone* was a competitor.

When Leah finished sewing ribbons on her shoes, Kay was still nursing her ankle. "How'd you like Diana's class?" Leah finally asked her, dying for some feedback on the difficult teacher. Today Patrick and Diana had traded groups. Leah had gotten through Patrick's session without one correction. He hadn't said a thing to the new girls, though he had been really tough with Alex during center work. At the end of class Leah had left trying not to gloat too much.

Kay grimaced. "Before I turned my ankle, I would have said I loved it."

"Pam must have loved it," Katrina interjected, a sparkle lighting her soft brown eyes. "Diana told her she had great ballon. She does, too."

Leah's throat tightened. Patrick's class had given her hope. Hearing of Diana's compliment to Pamela upset her. She felt a strong twinge of jealousy toward the southern girl. All anyone around here seemed to be talking about was Pam's great jump and her ability to hang in the air as if she had wings. Leah's jealousy quickly turned to anger toward Diana. What right had Diana to compliment Pam and make a fool of her? The answer sprang instantly to mind. Every right, of course. Pamela was obviously a better dancer than Leah and certainly deserving of praise. *All of the girls here are wonderful dancers and there are probably others as good or better than you,* Leah told herself. *You'd better prepare yourself to face it.* She bent low over her bag of shoes and wiped away a tear that threatened to roll down her cheek. She sat up, looking grim, but at least no one could see that she had almost started crying.

"Hmmmm—" Kay went on, continuing to describe the class, her eyes focused on threading a needle. "That's the only compliment Diana gave all day. She didn't even bother to correct a soul. My teacher back home wouldn't like that. But I liked her combinations better than Patrick's."

Linda agreed. She pulled a brush through her thick black hair and nodded. "Patrick's stuff all felt like I'd done some version of it before. Diana was more challenging. I bet she's a good choreographer." She met Leah's eye and gave her an apologetic smile. "I know she was tough on you, but I'd put that right out of my mind if I were you. Being so upset about a single correction like that's going to get in the way of your dancing, Leah. Anyway, Diana's not the judge around here. Madame Preston is. Besides, yesterday was yesterday, and tomorrow's a whole new ball game."

Leah sighed. Linda was right. Feeling jealous of Pamela wasn't going to help her.

"This is an audition." Madame Preston's cultured voice rang clearly across the Green Studio.

Behind Leah a girl groaned softly, and said in a tough New York City accent, "Cut the talk and let's start dancing!"

In spite of her nerves Leah almost laughed. She didn't know the girl's name but she had gotten a glimpse of her as they took their places for class. The girl's dainty sylphlike looks contrasted sharply with her streetwise voice.

Madame Preston stared in Leah's direction. Leah cringed under the steely gaze of the school's director. Madame Preston definitely had charisma. When she was young she must have been very beautiful. Even now with her steel-gray hair, piercing gray eyes, and straight, elegant nose, she was striking. She had to be nearly seventy, but she stood tall and straight as a slender sapling. Leah vowed to check the library's photo collection to see what Alicia Preston looked like when she had danced her famous role as the Lilac Fairy in the Royal Ballet's *Sleeping Beauty*.

Madame Preston cleared her throat and began

again. The room was quiet, except for the sound of breathing. "An audition means competition." The students all shifted uncomfortably and eyed one another. Leah knew the guilt she saw on each girl's face was mirrored on her own. She suddenly felt terrible about her feelings toward Alex and Pam.

"But you're not competing against Sue or Mary Ellen, or Vanessa or Samantha," the teacher continued, picking out names at random. "You're competing against the only real competition you will ever have to worry about." She paused for effect and folded one slender, well-manicured hand over the other. She lowered her voice to almost a whisper, but her words rang out clear as a bell. *"Yourselves."*

Leah leaned forward a little, still holding on to the barre.

"If you keep paying attention to other dancers while you're here for an audition, if you end up in our program, if you go on to dance somewhere else you will still get nowhere. To be a good dancer you have to learn to be yourself. To be a great dancer you will have to learn to let other people be themselves."

Leah's brow furrowed. At Madame Preston's next words she gasped. "Margot Fonteyn—who was a very great dancer—said that for her, competition did not exist. She couldn't afford to let it. She couldn't afford to let the petty jealousies, feuds, and rivalries so notorious in the dance world bother her. Because if you have all that anger and hatred and bitterness in your heart, you cannot go onto the stage and make beautiful art. Ballet is about making beautiful art. Those aren't her exact words, but I think you get my point."

Leah drew in a sharp breath. Miss Greene had told her that a hundred times, yet after only three days here at SFBA she had forgotten every word of that advice. Her attitude toward Alex, her feelings about Pam—it all felt so small and silly now. Leah caught Madame Preston's eye and for a second the director held her glance. Her gaze seemed to penetrate to Leah's very soul. Leah dropped her eyes and felt ashamed and made a solemn promise she would never let anger or jealousy or fear of another ballerina interfere with her dancing again.

Alicia Preston slowly walked from one side of the sunlit room to the other, her slippered feet making barely a sound on the smooth wood floor. She leaned against the window and looked out. No one in the room moved a muscle. Slowly she turned around. Leah felt as if she were watching a carefully polished performance. Not one gesture seemed excessive, exaggerated, or out of place. At the same time, nothing about her was stiff; every movement she made seemed natural. *She must have been a remarkable dancer once,* Leah thought.

"Today is the first phase of your examination. I will give you a class," Madame Preston continued briskly. "A class suitable for girls of your age and training. I will correct you as if you were in one of my regular classes, though I may get your names wrong." She started the class with a pleasant laugh. Leah giggled at the joke along with the other girls and glanced self-consciously at the name tag and number she had pinned to the front of her leotard.

Madame Preston turned away from the class and made a gesture toward the pianist. With graceful hand motions she demonstrated the opening sequence of pliés at the barre, and the class began.

When it ended, Leah had completely forgotten about the judges and their scribbling pencils and hushed comments. She walked out of the studio feeling as if she were walking on air. She had aches in parts of her body she'd never been aware of before. But none of that mattered. While the rest of the girls talked and whispered and complained about the class, trying to second-guess the judges' decisions, Leah remained silent. She secluded herself in the corner of the changing room and mentally reviewed each of the corrections Madame Preston had made. Every one of them had made sense, was brief and to the point, and Leah had the feeling that if she got the chance to study with the director, she might become a real dancer after all.

And even if she didn't make it into SFBA, after one class with this extraordinary teacher, she knew she'd never dance the same again.

Chapter 11

"Alex, you're out of your mind!" Kay said for the third time in ten minutes. Her hands shook as she tugged up her leg warmers and paced nervously back and forth in front of the barre that ran the length of the small practice room adjacent to the sumptuous Blue Studio. Music from *Giselle* seeped through the closed door, and a group of girls clustered around a tear in the shade, trying to sneak a peek at Sally Jenkins's audition. Leah didn't want to watch. She already knew Sally couldn't possibly dance *Giselle*. Her teacher must have been crazy to let her attempt it. She didn't want to see Sally—or anybody else—fail right now.

"It would have been better to put this whole thing off another day," Kay continued irritably. "Getting something bad over with fast is good for some people. But not for me," she said with a determined shake of her head. Tendrils of dark curls escaped from her bun and trailed along the back of her neck.

Leah didn't agree with Kay. For once she actually agreed with Alexandra. Alex had made a big thing last night, after the audition schedule had been announced, of telling everyone how good it was to go first. Even though you had that extra day's suspense before the acceptance list was posted on the call-board, you got the bad part over with fast. It was like taking vile-tasting medicine, she said. You drink it fast and *poof!* you're done with it. Leah agreed. She'd be happy to get the most nerve-racking part of the audition over with as soon as possible although she didn't know how she'd stand waiting for the results. She'd never been good at waiting.

She was even having trouble waiting her turn to appear before the judges. She dreaded the awful moment when she'd have to walk through that door to face Madame Preston and perform her variation. If it were only over with already! She grinned at her reflection in the mirror, trying to see if her teeth were clean. Miss Greene had told her to be sure to smile no matter what happened. Just smile, forget about the blisters on your toes, and look like life is a bowl of peaches and cream.

Leah pushed up the sleeves of her leotard and tackled her hair for the third time in ten minutes. She had warmed up twice already. While she was practicing her chaînés her hair had come undone. Now with only minutes before her own audition she was left with the hopeless task of getting it all pinned back up securely and neatly.

"Here, let me." Alexandra stepped up behind her and produced a stiff hairbrush out of her back pocket. With deft firm strokes she smoothed out Leah's hair and yanked an elastic through it. "You've got beautiful hair," she said, meeting Leah's eyes in the mirror.

"Thanks," Leah mumbled as Alexandra's skilled hands formed her hair into an attractive bun in a matter of seconds.

"You're welcome," Alex said in her usual arch tone. Then she spotted a girl across the room having trouble with her shoes. "What you need is some glue," Alex called as she crossed the studio in a couple of long strides. Leah couldn't get over the way the Russian girl oozed competence. Whenever someone needed help today, Alex was there. In the flurry of pre-audition warm-ups, a million little disasters had already taken place in the anteroom to the Blue Studio. Alex had transformed herself into a one-girl Red Cross brigade, bailing the other kids out of last-minute problems again and again.

Leah thoughtfully gnawed her lip. She had been wrong about Alex. Sorokin's style was brusque, and her accent made her seem aloof and distant, but watching the tall Russian girl, Leah felt a sharp twinge of regret. The past days she'd been downright cold to Alex, and she wished she could take that all back. Alex was beginning to seem like someone she'd like to have as a friend, assuming she got in to SFBA and got to see her again.

Leah leaned her elbows on the barre and did a few pliés. The butterflies in her stomach were getting out of hand now. No matter how many deep breaths she took, she couldn't calm down. After yesterday's class with Madame Preston, Leah's ambition to make the grade at SFBA had soared. The trouble was, her confidence hadn't.

The door to the studio burst open and Sally walked into the practice room. The tears streaming down her face told the whole story. She had received the ultimate rejection. Halfway through her variation Madame Preston had stopped her, thanked her, and told her to go home. Leah looked around the room helplessly. Kay was standing whitefaced by the studio door. She was next. Leah hesitated a moment, trying to decide if Sally or Kay needed her more. Alex was handing Sally tissues. Pam leaned arrogantly back against the barre, staring at Sally with an I-told-you-so look on her face. Leah's stomach clenched. Pam's true colors were beginning to show, and they weren't very pretty. Leah remembered how deftly Pam had put Kay's dancing down that first night at the coffeehouse. Well, Pam wasn't going to be able to say "I-told-you-so" about Kay. To make sure of that, Leah tugged up her leg warmers, marched up to Kay, and squeezed her hand.

"Go to it, Larkin. I know you'll be great," she said fervently, trying to bolster Kay's confidence.

"Thanks!" Kay said, her voice squeaking out. Then she walked into the Blue Studio and shut the door behind her.

Leah pressed her nose to the chink in the shade. Alexandra was close behind her. Out of the corner of her eye Leah could see Pam craning her neck trying to get a better view.

Inside the studio, Madame Preston sat behind a long mahogany table talking to Kay. Two other judges sat there making notes. Madame Preston motioned toward the pianist. Everyone waited for Kay to assume her opening pose. Slowly and deliberately, she crossed the room.

"Good going, Kay!" Alex congratulated under her breath.

Kay put her feet in a perfect fifth. The music started and her small body sprang to life. The dance was filled with quick, tiny hops and fast beats. Her feet looked like a hummingbird's wings as she skimmed across the floor, springing into one intricate series of jump and turns after another. Leah whistled under her breath. Kay was certainly the fastest dancer she'd ever seen.

"Oh, no!" Alex cried out, grabbing Leah's arm. A split-second later Kay fell flat on her behind right in front of the judges' table. She had been moving so swiftly, Leah didn't even see what she had done wrong.

"Get up!" Alex urged from behind the door. "Just *get up!*"

Kay couldn't hear her, but she scrambled quickly to her feet. Her face was red and her lips were trembling, but she somehow picked up her variation right on cue and finished it perfectly.

"I don't know why she bothered to finish," Pamela sneered. "Girls ten times better than her have failed without messing up half that much."

Leah whirled around and gaped at Pam. At that moment she knew she never wanted to talk to Pamela Hunter again.

Alex stomped her foot hard. "Pamela," she said icily. The sneer in her voice matched Pam's. "Just shut up. All you want is for everyone else around here to fail so you look good."

For once Pam was speechless. She glared at Alex for a long moment, then shrugged as if she didn't have a care in the world. She elbowed her way past Leah back toward the mirror, where she posed in a graceful arabesque and studied her reflection. Reaching up with one pale, soft hand, she preened her red hair like some exotic jungle bird.

Leah watched her, fascinated. Alex was right. Pam *did* want everyone else to fail. That was her game. Leah was astounded that she hadn't figured that out until now. Pam's continuous putdowns of other dancers suddenly made sense.

The door flew open and Kay practically soared in. She rushed toward Alexandra and reached out an arm for Leah. "They didn't say no. I even fell." She grimaced and rubbed her behind comically. A lovely laugh bubbled from her mouth.

"We saw!" Pam muttered sourly from the corner. She had stopped preening and was staring at Kay in her condescending way.

Kay didn't seem to hear her. "But they didn't say no. Not yet. They told me results would be posted Friday on the call-board." She wrapped her arms around her chest and gave herself a happy hug. "It's funny, but falling didn't really matter."

"But getting up did," Leah said warmly, meeting Alexandra's eyes. For a moment she was so proud of Kay, she forgot all about herself and her own nervousness.

Patrick poked his head in the door. "Pamela Hunter!" he called. "You're next."

Pamela straightened up and followed Patrick out of the room. The door closed behind her and Linda said what everyone else was thinking. "I'm not even going to wish her good luck."

"And she's going to need it. I didn't see her practice one step of her variation," Katrina said with a puzzled shake of her head.

Neither had Leah. It was odd. For the past forty minutes everyone who hadn't auditioned yet was warming up, practicing steps, trying to iron out the bad spots before the final showdown. Maybe Pam wasn't as smart as she thought.

Leah was tempted to watch Pam do her flashy variation. As much as she had begun to dislike Pam, she had seen enough of her dancing in Madame Preston's audition class to be very impressed. But Leah's turn was next. She resolutely walked to a corner of the room and carefully began warming up her feet. Her variation required lots of intricate pointe work, and she'd been waiting so long for her number to come up, her muscles were beginning to get cold.

She was in the middle of some echappés when Pam's music started. Leah was concentrating so hard on remembering the choreography to her piece that she thought the familiar melody was coming from inside her head. But then a look of horror crossed her face. "I don't believe it!" she cried in a tremulous voice. She ran across the room elbowing the other girls out of her way. She practically yanked Linda from in front of the door. "That's my variation!" she cried, her voice rising. "She can't really be doing this. She just can't!" Leah's hands flew to her face and she looked around at the other girls. Events of the past few days flashed before her eyes: the tapes; Pam's weird behavior in the library; that crazy story about Pam's date. Everything came into painfully sharp focus. Pam had seen Leah dance her variation and for some crazy reason she had decided to steal it.

Any minute now she would wake up and this would just be some part of a terrible dream. Not only was Pam performing Leah's solo, but she was performing it right before Leah was due to audition herself. No one else had danced it yet. And Pam was supposed to be doing *La Bayadère*. Everyone knew that. For a mad moment Leah thought of dancing something else. She tore away from the door and frantically searched through her dance bag. She had brought some extra ballet music along, just to study at the piano if she had had the time: the first act variation from *Giselle,* and a solo from the pas de trois in *Swan Lake*'s first act. Her hands shook as she pulled the yellowed sheet music out of a folder.

"What are you doing?" Alexandra demanded.

Leah looked up with terrified eyes. "I'll dance something else. That's all. I'm studying these. I can't go on after her. Not dancing the same thing. They won't even look at me. I think I know at least the bit from *Giselle* well enough. Robert's a good enough pianist to pick up the music."

Alexandra stared at Leah in disbelief.

"Do something new? Something you haven't rehearsed?" Kay said incredulously.

"Of course they'll look at you," Katrina broke in. She knelt down by Leah's side and gently smoothed a wisp of hair back from her forehead.

"You'll look like a dream compared with her!" Linda snorted. "She's dancing like a horse. Check it out!"

Leah looked from one face to the next. She walked back over to the window. Pam didn't look like a horse. She looked terrific. Her strong, athletic body didn't do justice to the delicate steps, but she made them look like a piece of cake. Leah shook her head. "I can't do it. I can't go on after her!" A sob rising in her throat choked her off. She turned to the wall and buried her face in her arms.

Alex clamped her hands down firmly on Leah's shoulder. "Stop it, Leah. *Now.*"

Leah looked up, her eyes smoldering. "Well, what would you do?" she practically shouted. She knew she was getting hysterical, but she couldn't control herself.

"I'd go out there and show those judges what a wonderful dancer you are. I'm sure Madame Preston has noticed already. I'd forget about Pam, and whatever she's doing to that solo."

"That's easy for you to say," Leah cried out. "You've got nothing to worry about. You're a student here already. You probably didn't even need to audition. After all, you're a Sorokin!" Leah bit her lip to keep from saying more. She didn't mean the words she'd just spoken in anger, but she felt the need to lash out at someone, at anyone. Pam was untouchable right now, but Alex was standing right in front of Leah, acting once again as if she had the answer to everything.

"That's not fair," Alex said softly. "But I don't blame you for being so upset. Leah, listen to me," she pleaded. "Listen to me. Pamela Hunter's not worth this. It's true she's not a very nice person, but she didn't steal your variation. You don't own it. No one does. If she wants to play some crazy game with the judges and with your head, that's her business. Yours is to go out there in front of the judges and dance your absolute best. So forget about her. You're reacting just the way she wants you to. Don't let her get the best of you. You know she wants you to fail just as she wants everyone here today to fail. Why do you think she puts everyone down all the time? Why do you think she tried to make you and Kay late for rehearsal? Why do you think she's trying so hard to be friends with James?"

Leah gasped at Alex's last remark. "James told me about how she was hanging on to him the other day," Alex explained. "That girl is ruthless. She wanted to be sure you didn't get a chance to get to know the best male dancer in this school. Pretty smart, huh?"

"But why is she out there dancing my steps, doing my variation?"

Leah sniffed back a tear as Linda handed her a

wad of tissues. She dabbed at her eyes carefully, trying not to smear her makeup.

"Because you're the biggest threat." Suddenly Leah knew Alex admired her, was maybe even a little bit jealous of her. She realized she felt the same way about Alex—impressed, yet afraid she'd never be quite as good. Only if she got into SFBA would she have the chance to find out if she could be impressed with, a little jealous of, and friends with someone all at the same time.

"Now get over to the barre," Alex ordered Leah. "You've still got two minutes to warm up. From this moment on, Pamela Hunter does not exist. *Poof!*" She snapped her fingers in the air as if she were doing a magic trick. The other girls laughed, relieved that the tension had been broken.

Leah closed off the rest of the world for the next few minutes and prepared herself to dance.

Chapter 12

Leah stepped into the Blue Studio as if she were walking onto the stage of the War Memorial Opera House. She was conscious of every part of her slender, well-proportioned body as she approached the judges' table.

She met Madame Preston's penetrating gaze without looking away. The regal director was dressed in a silvery lilac-colored suit and she looked incredibly cold and remote. "Would you like to warm up a bit first?"

"No," Leah replied. Her voice was very steady, though slightly hoarse from crying. She knew her eyes were red, but there was nothing she could do about that now except dance so well that Madame and the other judges wouldn't notice. Madame Preston cocked her head and studied Leah's face. Leah misunderstood her concern. "I warmed up inside the small studio. Like the other girls," she added quickly.

With an elegant sweep of her hand Madame Preston gestured toward the piano. Leah walked over to the left-hand corner of the studio and looked Robert in the eye. His thin lips parted in an encouraging, crooked smile. Leah responded with a barely perceptible nod of her head, and a second later the music began.

For the first few steps Leah's smile felt forced. She could hear Miss Greene's voice calling out the names of the steps in her head. Pretending she was in class practicing with her familiar life-long teacher helped her through the first few bars of music. Then something clicked inside her. Leah's mind's eye flashed on the tape of Fonteyn. She pictured the delicate, always perfect carriage of her head, the way she brushed the edge of her tutu with her hand as she performed the intricate series of piqués and hops. Suddenly Leah imagined away her plain black leotard. Suddenly she saw herself dressed in a sparkly white costume, a tiny rhinestone tiara on her head. She was a princess in a fairy tale, just awakened from an enchanted sleep and about to marry the prince of her dreams. During the pretty port de bras that was the signature of the piece, she looked at each of her hands in turn as they inscribed small circles in the air.

Before she knew it, she was whirling through the closing series of chaînés and piqué turns, each one more joyous and free than the next.

She held her closing arabesque a long time, a little longer than she had rehearsed with Miss Greene, but long enough for the audience, if there had been one, to burst into applause.

She stepped gracefully off pointe, pretending she was still onstage. She inclined her head to the pianist as she had been taught, then dropped into a classical curtsy in front of the judges' table. She felt terrific, as if she might just float out of the room, so certain was she that she had danced the best performance of her life. She finally dared to look up into Madame Preston's eyes.

That night at the stroke of eleven Leah was called to the phone. No one in the boardinghouse was asleep yet. Everyone was too up from their audition. With their adrenaline still flowing, none of them wanted to sleep. Sally had called out for pizza to celebrate her departure in the morning. Most of the girls had gathered in her room for this rare pigout, but no one had invited Pam.

Leah hurried down the stairs clutching her robe tightly over her nightgown. She licked a bit of cheese from the end of her thumb before picking up the receiver. "Hello," she said. Mrs. Hanson clicked down the extension.

"Uh, hi. It's me."

Leah leaned back against the wall. "Chrissy? Is it really you?"

"Gosh, it's only been two weeks and you don't even remember my voice!" Chrissy's laugh sounded forced, but Leah knew instantly her old friend was just trying to be funny. She wasn't angry at her for leaving San Lorenzo anymore. Leah wanted to sing at the top of her lungs. Everything really *was* all right. She had her best friend back again. Leah realized now how much she'd been missing her.

"I—I'm glad you called." Chrissy had never called

her first after an argument before. Leah gave a contented squirm and wound a strand of her hair around her finger. "So what's new?" she asked, picturing Chrissy in those awful camouflage cut-offs she'd worn all summer long, her feet propped up against the wall in the Morleys' upstairs hallway. "Nothing much—" Chrissy began. "Well, that's not quite true." Her voice made it obvious that she was bursting with news. "I tried out for—you're never going to believe this—"

"What? Come on, Chrissy, the suspense is killing me." Leah bounced up and down on her toes and put her hand over her mouth to stifle a giggle. Chrissy's voice dropped to a whisper on the other end of the phone. "I don't want my dad to know yet. He'll kill me. I tried out for *cheerleaders!*"

Leah was too shocked to respond.

"And I made it! All those dancing lessons finally paid off. I can jump higher than almost anyone on the j.v. squad. And guess what else?" Chrissy asked her friend. "I got contact lenses!"

"I don't believe this!" Leah finally gasped. So much had happened to Chrissy in the last two weeks.

"And one more thing."

From the ecstatic tone in Chrissy's voice, Leah knew exactly what was coming. "Your mother let you quit dancing."

"You got it!" Chrissy was exuberant. "I will never, ever set foot in the Hannah Greene School of Dance and Theater Arts again."

Leah laughed as she hadn't laughed in days.

Over the phone Chrissy laughed, too, the loud, boisterous chuckle that Leah had sorely missed.

"But, Leah." Chrissy sounded a little uneasy. "I actually called to wish you luck, and to tell you I'm sorry about our fight. I felt terrible about it. And I still want to be your best friend," she added in a joking voice. "I want to be the first person backstage when you get as famous as Makarova! I want to give interviews to the press and tell them about how I knew you way back when."

"Oooooh, you'd better not," Leah scolded, then grew serious. "It's my fault, too, Chrissy, and I'm sorry. And about that luck, well, I guess I still need it, but the audition was over for me today."

"What happened?" Chrissy asked breathlessly.

"You aren't going to believe this!" Leah lowered her voice and cast a glance toward Pam's room. The alcove off the living room was dark, and as far as she could tell, Pamela was asleep.

"Oh, Chrissy." Leah slid her back down the wall and sank down to the floor. She twirled the phone wire in her hand and shook her head ruefully. "I sure could have used you here this week to talk to. I just don't know how anything went. I'm not even sure what went on." Thinking over the complex events that had taken place over the last week made Hannah Greene's school and San Lorenzo seem like places out of a different world, a world that was wonderfully simple.

"Things have been really heavy here," Leah continued in a whisper. She told Chrissy about the new girls she'd met, about Alexandra, Kay, and the others. Then she told her all about Pam and her stealing her piece for the audition. "I'm so angry at her I could burst. Do you know that? If I could only think of some way to get back at her," Leah said, raising her voice louder than she intended. She bit her lip and cast another glance toward Pam's room to make sure nothing was stirring inside.

"Whoa." Chrissy chuckled into the phone. "I know what you're like when you're angry." Her voice grew more serious. "But she doesn't sound worth it to me. You can't let these things get to you, Leah. Revenge, my friend, has a way of worming its way into your heart. You've got too much dancing to do to get involved in that." In a lighter tone she added, "And anyway, you don't want to start looking like the bad guy, do you? Think of the roles you'll be stuck with then. All that heavy black and green makeup, nothing but dark costumes." She let out a cackle worthy of the soundtrack from a horror movie. She had seen *Swan Lake* with Leah once, and her favorite dancer was the guy who played the evil sorcerer named Von Rothbart.

Leah didn't say anything. She looked down at the figures in the carpet and traced the design with her bare toe.

"Leah?"

"Yes, Chrissy. I heard you. I don't really want to get revenge. Nothing like that. But I'm not sure I can just let it all go so easily."

"Well, think about it. Playing her game will just bring you down to her level," Chrissy warned.

"I'll think about it," she promised her friend. "And Chrissy—"

"What?"

"You know, you're right. I am going to make new friends here if I get in, but I'll never have another friend like you," she said with feeling. Then she gave an embarrassed laugh. "So when do I see you?" Leah asked. "I'll be back home Friday night."

"I'll be outside of People's Drugs. I'll bring the rest of the pom-pom girls. You'll recognize me. I'm the one whose hair clashes with the magenta pom-poms. The San Lorenzo High brass marching band will be there, too, and the mayor, and, of course, your mom."

"But what if I don't get in."

Chrissy burst out laughing. "Then we'll have to celebrate San Lorenzo's biggest flop!"

Leah joined in her friend's laughter and couldn't stop. The image of the whole high school band spread out on the lawn to greet her was a hilarious one. She was still laughing when she hung up, and she could hardly wait to see her old friend again.

"Shut up out there. I'm trying to get some sleep," Pam's angry voice drawled from the nearby bedroom.

Leah wrinkled her nose and stuck her tongue out in the dark. It was a childish five-year-old thing to do, but it made her feel so much better that at the foot of the stairs she turned around and did it again.

Chapter 13

"I'm in! I'm in!" Kay screamed at the top of her lungs and jumped up and down. The commotion in the front hall was incredible. Girls were crying, hugging each other, shrieking for joy. Others slunk off to hide their disappointment from the world. The list of the new SFBA students had just been posted. Katrina and Linda were on it, along with Kay. Kay looked around for Leah. Their eyes met and the smile faded from Kay's face. Leah was pale and her bottom lip trembled. "If I made it, I know you did," she practically shouted into Leah's ear. She shook Leah's shoulder. "It's just not possible that you didn't," she said, sounding a little hysterical.

Leah couldn't say a word. A sob rose to her throat. She tapped the neatly typed list with her finger. Through her tears she could barely make out the alphabetically arranged names. But she had read it three times already, almost sure she had made a mistake. But she hadn't. Picchi, Remington, Ryan, Silva, Thomas. The alphabet skipped right over Stephenson. She poked through the contents of her pocket and pulled out a tissue. Looking over at Kay she tried to smile. "I—I'm glad—for you."

Someone grabbed her arm from behind and shook her hard. Leah whirled around. Alex was standing there shaking her head in disgust. "You may be a smart dancer but you're definitely a very dumb girl!" She put her hands on either side of Leah's head and forced her to face the bulletin board. "Look," she said.

"Stop it, Alex!" Leah cried, pulling loose from her grasp, but not before she saw the reason Alex was smiling. Out of alphabetical order and at the bottom of the list were two more names. She read them aloud. "Leah Stephenson; Pamela Hunter." Next to each name was an asterisk. At the bottom of the page was a little note for her and Pamela to be in the Blue Studio in a half hour in practice clothes.

Leah's hopes soared into the stratosphere for an instant, then abruptly crashed. "What does this mean?" she whispered, meeting Kay's eyes, then Alexandra's.

Alexandra toyed with the large silver pendant dangling around her neck. "I don't know," she said slowly. "I've been here two years and I've never seen anything like this before. But I don't think it's bad news. You're on the list, you know. That means you're in!"

Leah wasn't so sure of that. Her name *was* on the list, but so was Pam's. Right there at the bottom. But the asterisk and note made acceptance sound so tentative, as if she still had something to do to prove herself a good enough dancer for the Academy. Leah wasn't sure she had the strength left for whatever it was.

"Good luck!" Alex and Kay cried out in unison as Leah grabbed her dance bag and bolted up the front stairs.

Pam walked into the warm-up studio a few minutes after Leah. They glanced at each other in the mirror without saying a word. Pam strutted to the farthest end of the barre and began her pliés. The haughty expression on her beautiful face didn't conceal her fear.

Leah forced her eyes away from the mirror. She took a deep breath and lifted her leg onto the barre. Exhaling, she stretched into a side bend, first away from her raised leg, then toward it. She closed her eyes so she couldn't see the panic she knew was written on her face.

At the stroke of two she walked into the Blue Studio. Yesterday, in spite of all the commotion and her nervousness, she had managed to enter the audition room with tremendous confidence. Today she could barely keep her knees from shaking. Halfway across the room she stopped and looked up at the table. Madame Preston was there along with Diana, Patrick, and a couple of other people she'd never seen before. They all sat behind the long mahogany table like some kind of grand jury. The only person missing was Robert. Leah frowned. Was she supposed to dance without music?

"To the barre, Leah," Madame Preston commanded.

Leah obeyed. She went to the one on the left wall. Whatever paces they had planned to put her through now, she might as well show off her stronger side first.

"Two grand pliés in fifth to the front, to the back, two demis, then repeat," Madame said.

Leah paused a moment and let her head fill with the opening bars of a Chopin étude. She hated to work just counting out the beat. It was always so much easier to move to the melody of the music.

"Enough!"

The music inside Leah's head clicked off.

"Now developpé to the front, side and back, on pointe please. Repeat on the other side."

Leah's face colored. Had Diana suggested she go through that routine again to show her up? Well, Diana was in for a surprise. Leah lifted her weight off her hips and imagined she was lighter than air, floating up like the wind but rooted fast to the ground like a tree or a rock. Listening to the tune inside her head, she danced the routine exercise in the silence of the room. This time there wasn't even the scribble of pencils.

"Walk over here, please," Madame Preston barked, "*slowly*!" A pulse began to throb in Leah's temple. What was this all about? If they didn't want her, why didn't they just come out and say so. She approached the table and glared at the director with fire in her eyes. Madame Preston didn't seem to notice. She regarded Leah coolly, looking her up and down as if she were a dress she was thinking of buying.

"What's your family situation?" Patrick asked her. His voice was kind and encouraging.

Leah returned his smile weakly. "I live with my mother. My father—he died when I was little," she said in an unsteady voice. The question surprised her and took her off guard.

"Can your mother afford to send you to the Academy?" Madame Preston inquired.

Leah frowned. She had already filled out all the financial forms. Why were they asking all these dumb questions? "Yes. Yes, she can," she replied impatiently.

One of the men Leah didn't recognize spoke up. "Where have you studied? Who is your teacher?" He had a crisp British accent. He peered at her from behind black-framed glasses with narrowed blue eyes. Leah decided he must have been very handsome when he was young.

"Miss Greene's School of Dance and Theater Arts." Madame Preston leaned out over the table and answered the man's question before Leah had a chance. She sounded almost as if she were about to start laughing. Leah clenched her hands into tight little fists as Madame said, "*Hannah* Greene's School of Dance and Theater Arts."

"Ah, no wonder." The man studied Leah closely. "That explains a lot. Hannah, Miss Greene, had a very great teacher herself. We danced together sometime back. I had lost track of her. I must look her up while I'm working here at the school. I had forgotten she lives in the region. She's a very talented woman." Leah stared at the man. He was probably around Miss Greene's age and he looked as if he had once been a dancer. She wondered who he was. He watched her stare at him, then smiled. She recognized him instantly. "You're Christopher Robson, Miss Greene's partner. There's a picture of both of you on the wall in her office." The words spilled out of her before she remembered where she was. Her hands flew to her mouth and she blushed furiously. "Sorry!" she mumbled, casting an apologetic look at Madame Preston.

To her amazement the director smiled back at her. When she smiled, she looked remarkably like Mrs. Hanson. Leah swallowed hard, dropped her hands to her sides, and tried to stand tall.

For a moment no one said anything. Leah couldn't stand the suspense one minute longer. "Can't you tell me why I'm here?" she suddenly cried, resting her hands on the table. "Did I get in?" Her eyes pleaded with Diana to say something. Diana gave Leah a puzzled look. But Madame Preston spoke up first.

" 'Get in?' " she repeated. "My dear child, of course you got in!"

Leah's mouth fell open. "Then what am I doing here?" She heard the frustration in her own voice, then suddenly felt embarrassed.

Madame Preston was the director of the school; of course she could ask Leah to come in front of a group of people and do pliés. She could ask her to stand on her head and recite the alphabet backward if she wanted to. And Leah didn't doubt that she would do it. She'd do anything for Madame Preston at that moment. She had gotten in!

She was really going to go to SFBA with Alex, Linda, Katrina, and Kay. Her eyes shone as she looked from Madame Preston to Diana to Christopher Robson and the other two men at the table. "Oh, thank you!" she exclaimed, clasping her hands together and forcing back tears of joy that threatened to spill from her eyes.

Madame Preston regarded Leah quietly for a moment. Finally, she cleared her throat and said, "I apologize if you were so worried. I should have told you first. I just wanted these members of our board of directors to see you."

Madame Preston leaned back in her chair and looked directly at Leah. "You are a very gifted dancer, Ms. Stephenson."

Leah's heart soared. She was surprised to find her feet were still on the ground.

"One of the best to come along here in a while. Sorokin's another. But your gift is a very great responsibility. Things come easy to you that are hard for other girls. But you must work even harder to do what other girls find impossible. Do you understand?"

"I—I think so." Leah gulped. At the moment she wanted to sing and stamp her feet and laugh and dance for joy and shout out the window to tell the whole world Madame Preston had told her she had a gift. Instead, she clasped her hands together tightly and stood very still.

"So we will work you harder than the other girls, push you further."

Leah's eyes met Diana's. Diana flashed her a warm smile.

Madame Preston continued. "If you're lucky, you might actually make something of yourself." From the tone of her voice Leah knew the director was finished with her. She was dismissed.

She moistened her lips and whispered, "Thank you very much." She didn't think she'd ever meant anything quite as sincerely.

She turned around and forced herself not to race out of the room.

"Oh, I almost forgot," Christopher Robson called after her. "Now and then we give a small scholarship. The Golden Gate Award. I was called here to decide if any applicant should get it. It's not based on need. It's a merit award for a girl of unusual talent. We grant it only now and then. Ms. Sorokin has one. You'll have one now too. It will help with board, and toe shoes," he added with a twinkle in his eye.

"Oh, Mr. Robson, thank you," Leah cried as she scooted out the door, nearly running right into Robert. "I got in," she cried, and surprised herself by throwing her arms around the tall young man's skinny neck and hugging him hard.

"I know!" Robert said, stepping back a bit stiffly. Then he smiled. "I'm glad. You're a very musical girl." Leah sensed that was Robert's greatest compliment, and she glowed. He straightened his glasses and pushed up the knot of his tie before proceeding into the studio. Pam followed close behind. She didn't even deign to look at Leah as she brushed by.

Leah was too happy to care. She sat in the middle of the studio and yanked on her leg warmers. She'd change later. Right now all she cared about was running downstairs and announcing her news to the world. Leah stopped what she was doing and grinned at her reflection in the mirror. Not *the* world, but *her* world. She flopped down on her back and pictured Alexandra, Kay, Katrina, and the others. She had known them only a couple of days, but what days they had been! Each one had been packed with enough crazy emotions to last her a lifetime. And Leah had a feeling that all of her days for the next three years at SFBA were going to be just as difficult, just as crazy, and just as wonderful. Best of all, she had made at least two wonderful friends to share them with.

The sound of Robert's piano startled her. The brilliant music of the bravura variation from *La Bayadère* filtered into the room. The judges must have decided they needed to see Pam dance the variation she had originally chosen for her audition. Leah scrambled to her feet and tiptoed over to the door separating the two studios. Sure enough, Pam was leaping and jumping and whirling in the air with incredible lightness and grace. She had the best elevation Leah had ever seen in a girl. In fact, she outjumped some of the boys from the company who had been in class the past few days. There was a cold, hard brilliance to her movement. Leah remembered Pam saying she had wanted to perform the thirty-two fouettés from the coda of the Black Swan pas de deux, but her teacher had refused to let her do it as her audition. Leah figured the piece from *La Bayadère* really showed off her jump better. But someday Pam deserved to dance the equally bravura role of the Black Swan. The angry, haughty expression on the redhead's beautiful face perfectly suited the role of the evil swan maiden.

The music stopped. Leah stepped away from the door, but before she got out of the small studio, Pam stomped in. She marched over to the barre and grabbed her towel and dance bag. With one hand on the door leading to the dressing room, she turned around. Her eyes were flashing fire, and her face wore a mean, triumphant expression. "At least I got in dancing something worth dancing. Any fool can do what you did!" she spat out.

Bang! The door slammed behind her. Leah jumped. Her hand flew to her throat. Pam must really hate her to say something like that. Leah remembered Chrissy's advice of the night before: Stay away from her, don't cross her path, and mind your own business. But how could she ignore a comment like that? Leah's fist clenched, then her hand fell limp at her side.

Was Pam right? Had she taken the easy way out with her piece? Leah's head started pounding and the pressure built behind her eyes. She pressed her hands to her temples as if to push back all the fear and anger and doubt that threatened to flood out.

A burst of laughter filtered through the closed door. Madame Preston's clear, firm voice said something. Leah couldn't make out her words, but just the sound of them grounded her. She stood up straight and primly tucked her hair back into her chignon.

Pamela Hunter may have given an impressive performance at a second audition. But she, Leah Stephenson, had won the coveted Golden Gate scholarship, awarded to a student of exceptional promise and talent, regardless of need. Nothing Pam could do or say could take that away.

Leah faced the mirror and dropped a graceful curtsy. "You," she whispered to her reflection, "really did it. Not Pam. Not anyone else." All her hard work had paid off. Leah had one foot planted on the ladder leading upward to the stars of her dreams. No one could pull her down now.

She left by the side door, avoiding the dressing room. She'd get her clothes later. She ran swiftly down the broad spiral staircase into the hall. Alexandra and Kay were waiting, just as she knew they would be.

Her face was all smiles as she grabbed Alex by one hand, Kay by the other. She spun them around and around in a circle until all three were laughing and dizzy. "I did it!" she cried.

"I told you so!" Alexandra said smugly, her dark eyes glowing.

Kay dropped Leah's hands and bounced up and down on the ends of her toes. "And I've got even better news. We're all rooming together at Mrs. Hanson's."

Leah stared uncomprehendingly at Kay. "You mean that?"

"I checked the list. Your name was on it. Katrina's going to live with a host family a couple of blocks away. Linda's going to commute from her uncle's in Oakland until something closer opens up. But you'll be at Mrs. Hanson's."

"There's only one problem," Alexandra said grumpily. "Pam. She's at Mrs. Hanson's, too."

Leah's hands flew up as if to ward off a blow. "Don't, don't tell me about it now. I don't want anything to spoil this moment."

Even though she was still in her leotard and toe shoes, she pulled the girls with her through the open French doors onto the back lawn. The Golden Gate Bridge shimmered in the afternoon sun, and the fog was still banked far off shore. "This is the happiest day of my life, and I've got two wonderful new friends to share it with."

"Me too!" Kay said with a catch in her lilting voice. "And I hope we stay friends forever!"

Leah's eyes were wide with joy. She felt as if she were going to burst with it. "Yes," she said, looking from Kay to Alexandra. "Friends forever."

Alexandra's full lips turned up into a lovely smile. "Forever!" she repeated, stretching her arms out to the other girls in a wide expansive gesture.

Leah hugged them both and for no reason at all started laughing. Then Kay and Alexandra began laughing too. Their laughter soared high into the sky and floated out over the lush green grass, dissolving in the light of the bay.

GLOSSARY

Adagio. Slow tempo dance steps; essential to sustaining controlled body line. When dancing with a partner, the term refers to support of ballerina.

Arabesque. Dancer stands on one leg and extends the other leg straight back while holding the arms in graceful positions.

Ballon. Illusion of suspending in air.

Barre. The wooden bar along the wall of every ballet studio. Work at the barre makes up the first part of ballet class.

Battements. Throwing the leg as high as possible into the air to the front, the side, or the back.

Bourrée. Small, quick steps usually done on toes. Many variations.

Centre work. The main part of practice; performing steps on the floor after barre work.

Chaîné. A series of short, usually fast turns on pointe by which a dancer moves across the stage.

Corps de ballet. Any and all members of the ballet who are not soloists.

Developpé. The slow raising and unfolding of one leg until it is high in the air (usually done in pas de deux, or with support of barre or partner).

Echappé. A movement in which the dancer springs up from fifth position onto pointe in second position. Also a jump.

Fouetté. A step in which the dancer is on one leg and uses the other leg in a sort of whipping movement to help the body turn.

Pas de deux. Dance for two dancers. ("Pas de trois" means dance for three dancers, and so on.)

Piqué. Direct step onto pointe without bending the knee of the working leg.

Plié. With feet and legs turned out, a movement by which the dancer bends both knees outward over the toes, leaving the heels on the ground.

  Demi plié. Bending the knees as far as possible leaving the heels on the floor.

  Grand plié. Bending knees all the way down

letting the heels come off the floor (except in second position).

Pointe work.   Exercises performed in pointe (toe) shoes.

Port de bras.   Position of the dancer's arms.

Positions.   There are five basic positions of the feet and arms that all ballet dancers must learn.

Retiré.   Drawing the toe of one foot to the opposite knee.

Tendu.   Stretching or holding a certain position or movement.

Here's a look at what's ahead in CENTER STAGE, the second book in Fawcett's "Satin Slippers" series for GIRLS ONLY.

Kay jumped excitedly to her feet.

"In a few weeks we—at least some of us—" she corrected herself, "are going to perform on a real live stage, with dancers from the Bay Area Ballet."

Leah couldn't believe her ears. "You mean that?"

Alex looked less than impressed. "What kind of stage?"

Kay glared at Alex and explained with exaggerated patience. "Alex, I'm sure you've seen one or two in your day. You know, a place with spotlights, footlights, floorboards. We get to wear makeup. There's a real audience." She turned to Leah and continued enthusiastically, ignoring Alexandra's skeptical reaction. "I was helping with the filing in the office, and I couldn't help but overhear Patrick on the phone with someone from the California Council for the Arts. It turns out that students from the Academy are going to take part in a series of dance lectures and demonstrations at local high schools, and company members will be part of the show, too. I'm so excited."

"So that's all?" Alexandra was visibly disappointed. "That happens every year. I've taken part in it ever since I got here, and let me tell you, it's a lot of work. All these kids you dance in front of just blow bubble gum and talk and giggle, and the boys whistle." Her full mouth curved down with distaste. "They don't seem too interested in ballet." She gave a disgusted toss of her head and eyed the thick envelope in Leah's hand eagerly. Chrissy's news obviously appealed to her more than Kay's.

Leah sat back on her heels, her face lit up with a huge smile. Maybe dancing in front of a bunch of high school kids wasn't as big a deal as dancing on the stage of a real theater, but it was a beginning. "Oh, Kay, it's wonderful news. I can't wait. Who's going to be picked?" Will everyone get a chance to perform? Even first year students? And what are we dancing?" She shot her questions rapid-fire at Kay.

Kay let out a lovely laugh and shielded her face with her hands as if to ward off Leah's enthusiasm. "I don't have *all* the answers yet! Give me a chance." She looked around, then lowered her voice and beckoned the other girls closer. "I do know one thing, though. I heard Patrick, Diana, and that really cute new teacher, Evan Macaulay, talking it over: students—not company members—are going to be chosen to dance the balcony scene from *Romeo and Juliet*!"

Alexandra screeched. She grabbed Kay's arm and shook her fiercely. "Are you sure about that?"

Kay nodded and looked smug. She had just made Alexandra Sorokin lose her cool and that was pretty big news in itself. She sat back happily and related what she had overheard the teachers discussing. "They felt it would be fun for the audience to have kids their own age dancing a ballet about teenagers," she said in conclusion.

"Dancing Juliet would be so—so—" Alex looked eagerly from Leah to Kay and tried to find the right words. "It would be so perfect." She let out a long wistful sigh. "Last year when the company premiered the new production of *Romeo* at the Opera House, all I wanted to do was dance Juliet. I memorized every single step. I don't care who I get to dance it in front of, or with, or anything." Alex cut herself off, and looked embarrassed at her outburst. She sat up straight and brushed a speck of dust off her black stretch pants. "Well, that certainly is big news and I can't wait until the auditions," she said.

"Auditions?" Kay and Leah exclaimed in unison.

Alex gave a puzzled frown. "Well, of course. That's how they always pick roles around here. It's part of a dancer's training."

Kay looked skeptical. "But Patrick said they want to give lots of new students a chance to dance."

"Oh, they will. These dance demonstrations go on for months, through the whole school year. They put together a program and groups tour the schools. They'll probably have first and second and third casts. It is a good chance to perform, I guess. But I wouldn't even try out at this point if it weren't for *Romeo and Juliet*."

"I can't imagine anyone picking me for Juliet," Kay said, unable to mask the disappointment in her voice.

"Oh, I wouldn't say that," Alex responded. "Besides, there will be other parts. I'm sure they already have you in mind to perform some of those allegro steps you're such a whiz at."

Leah nodded, looking thoughtful. "That's probably right, but to be honest—" Leah met Alex's eyes and didn't flinch as she said, "I know I'd give anything to dance Juliet, too. Everyone's going to feel like that." There wasn't a challenge in her voice, just a simple statement of fact, but Kay got her drift instantly.

The tiny dancer let out a sigh. "We're always going to be competing for parts around here. I guess we'd better get used to it."

ABOUT THE AUTHOR

Elizabeth Bernard has had a lifelong passion for dance. Her interest and background in ballet is wide and various and has led to many friendships and acquaintances in the ballet and dance world. Through these connections she has had the opportunity to witness firsthand a behind-the-scenes world of dance seldom seen by non-dancers. She is familiar with the stuff of ballet life: the artistry, the dedication, the fierce competition, the heartaches, the pains, and disappointments. She is the author of over a dozen books for young adults, including titles in the bestselling COUPLES series, published by Scholastic, and the SISTERS series, published by Fawcett.